LIKE EVERY ORPHAN, I had heard stories about Obernewtyn.

It was used by parents as a sort of horror tale to make naughty children behave. But in truth very little was known about it.

Some said it was just like another Councilfarm, and that the master there had only sought labor for an area too remote to interest normal laborers. Others said Lukas Seraphim was himself afflicted in some way . . . while still others claimed he was a doctor and wanted subjects to practice on.

Those Misfits taken there were never seen again.

BOOKS BY
ISOBELLE CARMODY

✦

THE OBERNEWTYN CHRONICLES

Obernewtyn
The Farseekers
Ashling
The Keeping Place
Wavesong
The Stone Key
The Sending
Red Queen

✦

THE GATEWAY TRILOGY

Night Gate
Winter Door

✦

LITTLE FUR

The Legend Begins
A Fox Called Sorrow
A Mystery of Wolves
Riddle of Green

JSOBELLE
CARMODY

·OBERNEWTYN

Random House 🏠 New York

Copyright © 1987 by Isobelle Carmody
Cover art copyright © 2007 by Penguin Group (Australia)
Map copyright © 2008 by Penguin Group (Australia)

All rights reserved.
Published in the United States by Random House Children's Books,
a division of Random House, Inc., New York.

Random House and colophon are registered trademarks of Random House, Inc.

The text of this work was originally published by Penguin Books Australia Ltd, Camberwell, in 1987. Published here by arrangement with Penguin Group (Australia), a division of Pearson Australia Group Pty Ltd.

Visit us on the Web!
www.randomhouse.com/teens

Educators and librarians, for a variety of teaching tools, visit us at
www.randomhouse.com/teachers

Library of Congress Cataloging-in-Publication Data
Carmody, Isobelle.
Obernewtyn / Isobelle Carmody. — 1st Random House ed.
  p. cm. — (Obernewtyn Chronicles ; bk. 1)
Summary: When she is exiled to Obernewtyn after her psychic abilities are discovered, Elspeth encounters others with powers like her own and discovers dark secrets concerning the ambitious overlords who control the destinies of all the outcasts.
ISBN 978-0-375-85767-6 (pbk.) — ISBN 978-0-375-95767-3 (lib. bdg.)
[1. Orphans—Fiction. 2. Persecution—Fiction. 3. Human-animal communication—Fiction. 4. Extrasensory perception—Fiction. 5. Friendship—Fiction. 6. Science fiction.] I. Title.
PZ7.C2176Ob 2008   [Fic]—dc22   2008017139

Cover and map design by Cathy Larsen
Cover background artwork by Les Petersen
Cover photographs by Getty Images

Printed in the United States of America
10 9 8 7 6 5 4 3 2 1
First Random House Edition

for Brenda

✦ INTRODUCTION ✦

IN THE DAYS following the holocaust, which came to be known as the Great White, there was death and madness. In part, this was the effect of the lingering radiation rained on the world from the skies. Those fortunate enough to live on remote holdings and farms were spared destruction, though they had seen the skies whiten and had understood that it meant death. These people preserved their untainted land and families ruthlessly, slaughtering the hundreds of refugees who poured from the poisoned cities.

This time of siege was called the Age of Chaos and lasted until no one else came from the cities. Unaware that the cities were now only silent graveyards on endless black plains where nothing lived or grew, the most powerful farmers formed a Council to protect their community from further siege and to mete out justice and aid. Peace came to the Land.

But time proved that the remote community had not completely escaped the effects of the Great White. Mutations in both man and beast were high. Not fully understanding the reason for the mutations, the Council feared for the community and decreed that any man or beast not born completely normal must be burned. To remove any qualms people might have about the killings, these burnings took on a ritual air, and were used by the Council to remind the people of their fortune in being spared in the holocaust and the time of Chaos.

The Council appointed a fledgling religious order to perform the burnings. The order, called the Herder Faction, believed that the holocaust was punishment from God, whom they called Lud. Gradually, religious dogma and law fused, and the honest way of the farmer was seen as the only right way. Machines, books, and all the artifacts of the Beforetime were abhorred and destroyed.

Some resisted the rigid lore, but by now the Council had provided itself with a band of militaristic protectors, called soldierguards. Any who dared oppose the order were tried and burned as seditioners or were given the lesser charge of being unsafe and sent to work on the Councilfarms.

After some time, the Herder Faction advised the Council that not all mutancies were immediately apparent at birth. Such afflictions as those that attacked the mind could not be discerned until later.

This created some difficulty, for while the Council saw the opportunity to further manipulate the community, accusing anyone of whom they disapproved of hidden mutancy, it was more difficult to proceed with a ritual burning of someone who had been accepted as normal for most of his or her life. The Council eventually decreed that none but the most horribly afflicted of this new kind of mutant would be burned and the rest would be sent instead to the Councilfarms. A new name was devised for anyone with an affliction not apparent at birth—Misfit.

It was a dark and violent age, though the untainted land flourished and even began cautiously to extend its boundaries as the effects of the Great White began at last to wane. New towns were established, all ruled by the iron hand of the Council from its seat in Sutrium. So great was the death toll under Council rule that hundreds of children were left orphaned each year. The Council responded by setting up a network of orphan homes to house those unclaimed by blood relatives.

The community regarded the inmates of orphan homes with an abiding suspicion, since most were the children of Misfits or seditioners, and as such were considered dangerous.

PART I

◆

THE LOWLANDS

◆ 1 ◆

BEFORE FIRST LIGHT, we set out for the Silent Vale.

It was a half day's journey, and we were led by a tall gangling boy called Elii, who carried a small sword and two hunting knives at his belt. These were the clearest visible reminders that our journey involved danger.

Also traveling with us was a young Herder. He represented the true danger that lay ahead. Around our necks we wore the dull graymetal circlet that denoted our orphan status. This would protect us from robbers and gypsies, for as orphans we owned nothing. Normally the presence of a Herder would be enough to frighten off robbers, who feared the wrath of the powerful order.

But this was a very young Herder, little more than a boy, with golden bum-fluff on his cheeks. His eyes held characteristic Herder zeal, but there was a nervous tic in one of his eyelids. I guessed this was his first duty away from the cloisters; he seemed as nervous of us as of any supernatural dangers he might perceive. It was rumored that Herders had the ability to see the ghosts of the Old-timers flitting about as they had done in the terrible days when the sky was still white and radiant. This talent was said to be Ludgiven so they could warn of the dangers that lay in following the evil ways of the Beforetimers.

Our expedition to collect whitestick was considered perilous but important. The Council had ruled that only orphan homes could mine the rare substance, perhaps because orphans were the most expendable members of the community. Collection of the whitestick was fraught with danger, for the substance could only be found in areas verging on tainted, where the land had not long ago been untouchable. The whitestick was poisonous to the naked skin and had to be passed through a special process designed to remove its poisons before it was of any use.

Once cleansed, it was marvelously versatile, serving in everything from sleep potions to the potent medicines prepared by the Herders.

I had not been to the Silent Vale before. This was the Kinraide orphan home's area of collection, and it yielded high-grade whitestick. But the Silent Vale was considered dangerously close to the Blacklands, where the poisons of the Great White still ruled. It was even whispered there were traces of Oldtime dwellings nearby. I was thrilled, and terrified, to think I might see them.

We passed through a side gate in the walls of the Kinraide complex. The way from that door was a track leading steeply downward. Seldom traveled, it seemed a world apart from the neat, ordered gardens and paths within the orphanage. Bush creepers trailed unchecked from side to side, choking the path in places.

Elii chopped occasionally at the vines to clear the way. He was an odd boy. People tended to shun him because of his profession and because of his close connections with the orphan home, though he was no orphan. His father had worked in the same capacity and his grandfather before that, until they had died of the rotting sickness that came from prolonged exposure to the whitestick. He lived on the grounds at Kinraide but did not associate with us.

One of the girls in our party approached him. "Why not travel along the crevasse instead of going up this steep edge?" she panted.

For some way, we had been climbing a steep spur along one side of the rise. Northward the dale ran up into a glen of shadows.

"The path runs this way," Elii snapped, his eyes swiveling around to the rest of us, cold and contemptuous. "I don't want to hear any more whining questions from you lot. I'm the Lud of this expedition, and I say there'll be no more talk."

The Herder flushed at the nearly blasphemous mention of Lud's name, but the restraint in his face showed he had been warned already about the rude but necessary youth. Few would choose to do his job, whatever the prize in the end. Elii turned on his heel and led us at a smart pace to the crest of the hill. From the top, we could see a long way—the home behind us and beyond that the town center, and in front of us, far to the west, lay a belt of mountains, purpled with the distance. The boundary of untainted lands. Beyond those mountains, nothing lived. Hastily I averted my eyes, for no one understood all the dangers of the Blacklands. Even looking at them might do some harm.

The dawn came and went as we walked, a wan gray light seeping into the world. The path led us toward a pool of water in a small valley. It was utterly still and mirrored the dull overcast sky, its southern end dark in the shadow of the hills.

"I hope we are not going to swim that because it is in the way," said the same girl who had spoken before. I stared at her defiant face, still stained with the red dye used by Herders to mark the children of seditioners. Elii said nothing, but the Herder gave her a look that would have terrified me. A nervous young Herder is still a Herder.

We came to the pool at the shadowed end only to find the path cleaved to the very edge of the water.

"Touch this water not!" the Herder said suddenly in a loud voice that made us all jump.

Elii looked over his shoulder with a sneering expression. A little farther on, a cobbled border, crumbled in places and overrun with sprouting weeds, ran alongside the track. It was uncommon enough for me to wonder if this was from the Beforetime. If so, I was not much impressed, but the Herder made a warding-off sign at the border.

"Avert your eyes," he cried, his voice squeaking at the end. I wondered if he saw something. Perhaps there were faint impressions of Oldtimers fleeing along this very road, the Great White mushrooming behind them, filling the sky with deadly white light.

An eastward bend in the path led us around the edge of a natural stone wall, and there we suddenly came upon a thing that was unmistakably a product of the Oldtime. A single unbroken gray stone grew straight up into the sky like the trunk of a tree, marked at intervals with bizarre symbols, an obelisk of the ancient past.

"This is where the other Herders spoke their prayers to Lud," said Elii. "They saw no danger before this."

The young Herder flushed but kept his dignity. He made us kneel as he asked Lud for protection. The prayer lasted a very long time. Elii sighed loudly and impatiently. Making a final sign of rejection at the unnatural gray pedestal, the young priest rose and self-consciously brushed his habit.

The same girl spoke again. "Is that from the Before-time, then?" she asked. This time I did not look at her. She was dangerously careless and seemed not to think about what she was saying. And this Herder was nervous enough to report all of us because of the one stupid girl.

"It is a sign of the evil past," said the Herder at last, trembling with outrage. Finally, the girl seemed to sense she had gone too far and fell silent.

One of the others in our party, a girl named Rosamunde whom I knew only slightly, moved near and whispered in my ear, "That girl will be off to the Councilcourt if she keeps that up."

I nodded slightly but hoped she would not prolong her whispering.

To my concern, she leaned close again. "Perhaps she doesn't care if they send her to the farms. I heard her whole family was burned for sedition, and she only escaped because of her age," she added.

I shrugged, and to my relief, Rosamunde stepped back into line.

When we stopped for midmeal, Rosamunde sought me out again, sitting beside me and unwrapping her bread and curd cheese. I hoped there was nothing about her that would reflect on me. I had heard nothing of any detriment about her, but one never knew.

"That girl," Rosamunde said softly. "It must be un-bearable to know that her whole family is dead except for her."

Unwillingly, I looked to where the other girl sat alone, not eating, her body stiff with some inner tension. "I heard her father was mixed up with Henry Druid."

I pretended not to be interested, but it was hard not to be curious about anyone linked with the mysterious rebel Herder priest.

Rosamunde leaned forward again, reaching for her cordial. "I know your brother, Jes," she said softly. I stiffened, wondering if he had sent her to spy on me. Unaware of my withdrawal, she went on. "He is fortu-nate to be so well thought of among the guardians. There is talk that the Herder wants to make him an assistant."

I was careful not to let my shock show. I had heard nothing of that and wondered if Jes knew. He would have seen no reason to tell me if he did.

Jes was the only person who knew the truth about me. What he knew was enough to see me burned, and I was frightened of him. My only comfort lay in the ten-dency of the Council to condemn all those in a family tainted by one Misfit birth. Jes might not be burned, but he would not like to be sentenced to the Councilfarms to process whitestick until he died. As long as it was safer for him to keep my secret, I was safe, but if it ever appeared that I would be exposed, I feared Jes would denounce me at once.

Suddenly I wondered if he had engineered my in-clusion on the whitestick expedition. As a favored or-phan, he had some influence. He was too pious to kill me himself, though that would have been his best solution, but if I died seeking whitestick, as many did, then he would be innocently free of me.

Elii called us to move. This time I positioned myself near him, where Rosamunde would not dare chatter. The Herder priest walked alongside, muttering his incantations. We had not gone far when a rushing noise came through the whispering greenery. We arrived shortly thereafter at a part of the path that curved steeply down. Here a subterranean waterway, swollen with the autumnal rains, had burst through the dark earth, using the path as its course until the next bend.

"Well, now," Elii said sourly.

The Herder came up to stand uneasily beside him. "We will have to find another way," he said. "Lud will lead us."

Elii snorted rudely. "Your Lud had better help us on *this* path—there ain't no other way."

The priest's face grew red, then white. "You go too far," he gasped, but Elii was already preoccupied, drawing a length of rope from his pack and tying the end around a tree. Then he slung the other end down the flooded path.

The Herder watched these movements with a look of horror.

Elii pulled at the rope, testing it, before swinging agilely down to the bottom of the small waterfall. Back on dry ground, he called for us to do the same, one at a time.

"We'll be dashed to pieces," Rosamunde observed gloomily.

The Herder gave her a dark look as one of the boys started to climb carefully down. Several others went, then Rosamunde, then me. The rope was slippery now and hard to grip. I found it difficult to lift my own weight. Two-thirds of the way down, my fingers became too numb to cling properly, and I fell the last several handspans, crashing heavily into a rock as I landed. The water soaked into my trousers.

"Get her out. The water may be tainted," Elii growled, then yelled up for the priest to descend.

I was completely breathless and dazed from my fall, and my head ached horribly where I had hit it on the rock.

"She's bleeding," Rosamunde told Elii.

"Won't matter. Running blood cleans a wound," he muttered absently, watching the priest descend slowly and with much crying out for Lud's help. I felt as though I were watching through a mist.

When the Herder reached the bottom, he knelt beside me quickly and began reciting a prayer for the dead.

"She's not dead," Rosamunde said gently.

Seeing that I was only stunned, the priest bandaged the cut on my temple with deft efficiency, and I reminded myself again that for all his youth, the Herder was fully trained in his calling.

"Come on," Elii said impatiently. "Though I doubt we'll make it in time now."

"Was the water tainted?" I asked. I ignored Rosamunde's audible gasp. There was no point in caution if I died from not speaking out.

The Herder shook his head, and I wondered how he knew—though I did not doubt that he was right. Herder knowledge was wide-ranging and sometimes obscure, but generally reliable.

We walked quickly then, urged on by Elii. My head ached steadily, but I was relieved that it was only a bump and not a serious infection. I had a sudden vision of my mother, applying a steaming herb poultice to my head. How quickly the pain had subsided on that occasion. Herb lore was forbidden now, though it was said there were still those who secretly practiced the art.

I nearly walked into Elii, having failed to notice he had called a halt.

"Through the Weirwood lies the Silent Vale," he said. "If we are too late today, we will have to camp here and enter the Vale tomorrow."

"The Weirwood?" said someone nervously.

"It is dangerous to be out at night in these parts," the Herder said, "where the spirits of the Beforetime rest uneasily."

Elii shrugged, saying there would be no help for it if the sun had gone. He had his orders. "Perhaps your Lud will cast his mantle of protection over us," he added with a faint glimmer of amusement.

We entered the Weirwood, and I shivered at the thought of spending a night there. It had an unnatural feel, and I saw several in our group look around nervously. We had not walked far when we came to a clearing, and in the center of this was the ravine they called the Silent Vale. It was very narrow, a mere slit in the ground, with steps hewn into one end, descending into the gap. The light reached just a handspan or so into the ravine, and the rest was in dense shadow.

I understood now Elii's haste, for only when the sun was directly overhead would it light the Vale, and it was almost at its zenith now.

We entered the ravine and descended the slippery

steps fearfully. By the time we reached the bottom, I was numb with the cold, and we huddled together at the foot of the steps, afraid to move where we could not see. Moments passed and the sun reached its zenith, piercing the damp mists that filled the ravine and lighting up the Vale.

It was much wider at the base, and unexpectedly, there were trees growing—though they were stunted and diseased, with few leaves. A thick whitish moss covered the ground and some of the walls in a dense carpet. Where the moss did not grow, the walls were scored and charred, possibly marked by the fire said to have rained from the skies during the first days of the holocaust. A faint stench of burning still filled the air.

Elii handed out the gloves and bags for gathering the whitestick, instructing us needlessly to be quick and careful and never to let the substance touch our skin. Pulling on the gloves, we spread out and set to work, searching for the telltale black nodules that concealed the deposits of whitestick.

The bags were small but took time to fill, because the substance crumbled to dust if not handled carefully. Standing to ease my aching back once I had finished, I noticed that I had wandered out of the sight of everyone else. I could hear nothing, though the others had to have been quite near. I had noticed at once the aptly named Vale was oddly silent, but now it struck me anew how unnatural that silence was, and how complete. Even the wind made no murmur. It was as if a special kind of death had come to the Silent Vale.

"Are you finished?" Rosamunde asked, apologizing when I jumped in fright. "This place is enough to give even a soldierguard a taste of the horrors," she said.

Returning to where some of the others had gathered at the bottom of the steps, we heard voices nearby.

"What do they use this stuff for, anyway?" one asked.

"Medicines and such, or so they say," said another voice with a bitter edge. It was the voice of the outspoken girl marked with Herder red. "But I have heard rumors the priests use it to make special poisons and to torture their prisoners for information," she added softly.

Rosamunde looked at me in horror, but we said nothing. I was no informer, and I did not think Rosamunde was. But that girl was bent on disaster, and she would take anyone with her stupid enough not to see the danger. Better to forget what we had overheard.

I left Rosamunde with the others, going to examine a deep fissure in the ground. The Great White had savaged the earth, and there were many such holes and chasms leading deep into the ground. I bent and looked in, and a chill air struck at my face from those black depths.

Impulsively, I picked up a rock and dropped it in. My heart beat many times before I heard the faint report of impact.

"What was that?" cried the Herder, who had been packing the bags of whitestick.

Elii strode purposefully over. "Idiot of a girl. This is a serious place, not the garden at Kinraide. Throw yourself in next time and make me happy." I looked at my feet with a fast-beating heart. Twice now I had called attention to myself, and that was dangerous.

Suddenly there was a vague murmur from the ground beneath our feet.

"What was that?" the Herder cried again, edging closer to the steps.

"I don't know," Elii said with a frown. "Probably nothing, but I don't like it. After all, we are not far from the Blacklands. Come, the sun is going."

We ascended the steps in a single file. The Herder, who came last, kept looking behind him fearfully as if he expected something to reach out and grab him.

An air of relief came over the group as we threw off the oppressive air of the Vale. Fortunately, we had gathered enough whitestick, and we made good time on our return, reaching Kinraide early in the evening.

To my private astonishment, Jes was among those who met us, and he wore the beaten potmetal armband of a Herders' assistant.

✦ 2 ✦

"ELSPETH?"

It was Jes, and I willed him to go away. He knocked again, then stuck his head in the door. "How are you?" he asked with a hint of disapproval.

Anger overcame caution. "For Lud's sake, Jes, they're not going to condemn me because of a headache. If you think it looks suspicious, then why don't you report me?" I retorted, staring pointedly at his armband.

He whitened and shut the door behind him. "Keep your voice down. There are people outside."

I bit my lip and forced myself to be calm. "What do you want?" I asked him coldly. I knew I was being stupid, but I didn't care. Jes was the only one I could strike out at. And that, I thought, looking at his stiff face, was becoming increasingly dangerous.

"Maybe you don't care about being burned, but I do. Much as you scorn it, caution has kept us safe until now. No thanks to you," he added, and I was bitterly reminded that our plight was my fault. "A headache is nothing, but you know how little things are blown out of all proportion. It is a short step from gossip to the Councilcourt in Sutrium."

"You have been made an assistant," I said flatly, and

now he reddened. A look of pride mingled with shame came over his face. "How could you?" I asked him bleakly.

He clenched his jaw. "You will not ruin this for me," he said at last. "It is my sin that I do not denounce you. But you are my sister."

"You would not dare denounce me," I said. "Your own life would be ruined if it was known you had a Misfit for a sister. Don't pretend you care for me."

A queer flicker passed over his face, and I suddenly felt certain that this was the truth.

When he had gone, I lay back, my head aching dully, partly from tension. For all my bravado, I was afraid of Jes. There had been a time when we were close. Not so much when we were young, for he had been a dutiful son, and I too much of a wanderer to please anyone except my beloved mother. But after we had come into the orphan home system following the trial and execution of our parents, we had clung to one another. Jes had vowed then to have revenge on the Council and the Herder Faction for their evil work that day. He had wiped my eyes and sworn to protect me.

He had not known what that would entail. In those first years, we regarded our secretive behavior as a game. It was only as we grew older that we became increasingly aware of the dangers. Discovering the truth about myself made me more solitary than ever, while Jes developed a near obsession with caution. In those days, his one desire had been to get a Normalcy Certificate and get out, then ask permission to have me with him. But somehow we had drifted apart, till the bonds that held us were fragile indeed. I knew Jes had become fascinated with the Herder Faction and its ideas. But as an orphan, he would never be accepted into the cloister, so I had thought little of it.

Recently, we had fought bitterly over his explanations for why the Herders had burned our parents. I had called him a traitor and a dogmatic fool; he in turn had called me a Misfit. That he would even say the word revealed how much he had changed.

Aside from Jes, people thought my recent headaches and bouts of light-headedness were the result of my fall on the path to Silent Vale that day, and I let them. I'd intended to hide the pain altogether, but I had cried out in the night, and the guardians had come to hear of it. In the end, I told them of my fall, because I did not want them to speculate, and had been given light duties and some bitter powders by the Herder.

If not the fall, then the headaches might have been simply a reaction to a change in the weather, for winds from the Blacklands did cause fevers and rashes. But deep down, I knew they had nothing to do with either the fall or the weather.

I shook my head and decided to go for a walk in the garden, slipping out a side door into the fading sunset. Jes had called me a Misfit, and according to Council lore, that was what I was. But I did not feel like a monster. In a queer mental leap, I thought about my first visit with my father to the great city of Sutrium. We had gone all that way for the fabulous Sutrium moon fair, and we weren't alone. Everyone who could walk, hobble, or ride seemed to be on the road to the biggest town in the Land, bringing with them hay, wool, embroidery, honey, perfume, and a hundred other things to trade. They had come from Saithwold, Sawlney, Port Oran, Morganna, and even Aborium and Murmroth.

I had not known then that Sutrium was also the home of the main Councilcourt. That I had discovered on my grim second visit. There had been no fair then. It was wintertime, and the city was gray and cold. There were no gay crowds filling the streets, only a few people who had regarded us furtively as we passed in the open carriage, our faces stinging from the red dye. We had not known then that Henry Druid had only recently disappeared, fleeing the wrath of the Council, and that the entire community was fearful of the consequences, since many had known and openly agreed with the rebel. But what I did understand, even then, was the hatred and fear in the faces of the people who looked at us. I had felt the terror of being different that has never left me.

Shuddering, I thrust the grim memory away. Ludwilling, I would never see such looks again.

The time of changing was near, and I sighed, thinking it would be better for us both if Jes and I were sent this time to separate homes. The Herder told us that the custom of moving orphans around regularly from home to home had arisen to prevent friendships forming that could not be continued once leaving the system. But it was widely accepted that the changing was engineered to prevent alliances between the children of seditioners, which might lead to further trouble. And there was another effect, evident only when the time for the changing approached. No one knew where they might go and whom they might trust in the new home.

Even before the relocation, we learned to prepare mentally, withdrawing and steeling ourselves for the loneliness that would come until the new home was familiar, until it was possible to tell who could be trusted and who were the informers.

I looked up. It was growing dark, and soon I would have to go in. Fortunately, no one minded my wandering in the garden even on the coldest of days, but I never stayed out beyond nightfall—those dark hours belonged to the spirits of the Beforetime. I leaned against a statue of the founder of Kinraide. Here I was hidden from the windows by a big laurel tree, and it was my favorite place.

The moon had risen early, and the darkening sky made it glow. An unnatural weakness coursed through me. I felt a sticky sweat break out on my forehead and thought I was going to faint. The pain in my head made me stagger to my knees.

I tried to force the vision not to come, but it was impossible. I stared up at the moon. It had become a penetrating yellow eye. I knew that eye sought me, and I felt the panic rise within me.

Then, abruptly, there was only the pale moon. My headache was gone, as though it had been only a painful precursor to what I had just experienced. I shivered violently and stood up. I would not let myself wonder about the vision—nor the others that had preceded it. Jes had told me long ago, when we could still talk of such things, that only Herders were permitted visions. "You must not imagine that you have them," he had said.

But I did not imagine them, either then or now, I thought, and walked shakily back across the garden. Yet though I did not try to understand what they meant, a few days later the meaning forced itself on me.

✦ 3 ✦

MARUMAN CONFIRMED IT in the end.

It had been a cold year overall despite the occasional muggy days that came whenever the wind blew in from the Blacklands. Most often even spring days were bitten with pale, frosted skies, which stretched away to the north and south and over the seas to the icy poles of the legends.

Sometimes in the late afternoon, I would sit and imagine the color fading out to where there was no color at all, as if the Great White again filled the skies, its lethal radiance leaching the natural blue. But unlike that age of terror when night was banished for days on end, I fancied the Land would be permanently frozen into the white world of wintertime, the sea afloat with giant towers of ice such as those in the stories my mother had told.

"Stories!" Maruman snorted as he came up, having overheard the last of my thoughts. I smiled at him as he joined me beside the statue of the founder. I scratched his stomach, and he rolled about and stretched with familiar abandon.

He was not a pretty cat nor a pampered one. His wild eyes were of a fierce amber hue, and he had a battered head and a torn ear. He once told me he had fought a village dog over a bone and that the hound had cheated by biting him on the head.

"Never can trust them pap-fed funaga lovers," he had observed disdainfully. "Funaga" was the thought symbol he used for men and women. "And I'd no sooner trust a wild one anytime; it'd bite me in half at one go."

Maruman possessed a dramatic and fanciful imagination. I thought perhaps that old war injury was to blame. Occasionally his thoughts would become muddled and disturbed. During those periods, he could dream very vividly. He had undergone such a fit shortly after we had begun to communicate, only to tell me that one day the mountains would seek me. I had laughed because it was such a strange image.

Another time he had confessed a Guanette bird had told him his destiny was twined with mine. This bird was used throughout the Land as a symbol representing an oracle-like wisdom or a preordained order of things. If there were meaning and reason behind the symbol, they were lost to me. The actual bird was said to be extinct. Yet Maruman quite often attributed his insights or notions to the direct intervention of the mythical wise bird.

Maruman was, he often told me, his own cat. Not so much wild, he would point out, as unencumbered. He once observed that life with a master was doubtless very nice, but for all that, he preferred his own way. Having a master, he said, seemed to take the stuffing out of a beast. I reflected to myself that this was certainly true. Despite this, and with a touch of cynicism, I thought that part of Maruman's devotion to me was because I fed him.

There seemed little to love in this rude, unbalanced cat with an ear that looked half devoured. Yet there was a kind of wild joy about him that I could only envy, for I was far from free. If he had been human, I think he would have been a gypsy, and in fact he quite liked to visit the troupes that roved about. He told me they fed him scraps and sang rollicking songs and laughed more than other funaga.

The bond between Maruman and myself had been the catalyst through which I had discovered the full extent of my telepathic powers. He said it had been destiny, but I doubted it.

I had been seated right next to the statue of the founder when it happened. A scraggy-looking cat was stalking a bird. I would have ignored them both, except that I was so struck by the carelessness of the bird. I thought it almost deserved its fate. As I concentrated on the pursuit, I suddenly had the sensation of something moving in my head. It was the queerest feeling, and I gasped loudly.

Startled, the bird flew off with an irritated chirp. I had saved the wretched creature's life, and it was annoyed! It did not yet occur to me to wonder how I knew what the bird felt. Instead I noticed that the cat seemed to glare indignantly at me with its bright yellow eyes. I shrugged wryly, and it looked away and began to clean itself.

I had the notion it was only pretending to ignore me. Then I laughed, thinking I must have sat too long in the sun. The cat turned to face me again, and for a moment I imagined a glint of amusement in its look. I wondered if maybe Jes was right and I was going mad.

"Stupid funaga," said a voice in my head. I somehow

knew it was the cat and stared at it in shock. "All funaga are stupid." Again I had heard what it was thinking.

"They are not!" I answered without opening my mouth. Now it was the cat's turn to stare.

That first moment of mutual astonishment had given way to a curiosity about each other that had in time grown to an enduring friendship. Once we had overcome our initial disbelief and began to pool our knowledge, Maruman revealed that all beasts were capable of mindspeaking together as we did, sensing emotions and images as well as brief messages, though typically not so deeply or intimately. He said animals had been able to do so in a limited way even before the holocaust, which, interestingly, he, too, called the Great White.

I told him my one piece of knowledge about the link between animals and humans, gleaned from a Beforetime book my mother had read. It had claimed humans evolved from some hairy animals called apes, which no longer existed as far as I knew, but neither Maruman nor I could feel that was more than a fairy tale.

I had heard many stories about the Great White from my parents as a child, which were different than the stories told by the Herders once I entered the orphan home system.

I remembered little from my childhood, but Herder lessons about the Great White and Beforetime were driven into us during the daily rituals and prayers, exhorting us to seek purity of race and mind. The priest who dealt with such matters at Kinraide was old, with a sharp eye and a hard hand. His manner of preaching often reduced new orphans to screaming hysteria. He made the Beforetime sound like some terrifying concoction of heaven and hell, woven throughout with sloth, indulgence, and pride: the sins suffered by the Oldtimers. The holocaust itself was paraded as the wrath of Lud in all its terrible glory.

This fearful picture was tempered by the stories one heard from other sources, gypsies and traveling jacks and potmenders, who presented the Oldtimers to us as men who flew through the air in golden machines and could live and breathe beneath the sea. Those stories left little doubt that the Beforetime people had possessed some remarkable abilities, however fantasized and exaggerated the details had become.

Maruman had little to offer about the Beforetime. He had more to say about the Great White. Dismissing the Herder version, Maruman said the beastworld believed that men had unleashed the Great White from things they called machines—powerful and violent inanimate creatures set deep under the ground, controlled and fed by men. Beasts called them glarsh.

I questioned him as to how inanimate things could be violent or fed, but he could not explain this apparent paradox.

Maruman said he "remembered" the Great White, and though that was impossible, he wove remarkably frightening pictures of a world in terror. He spoke of the rains that burned whatever they touched, and of the charnel stench. He spoke of the radiant heat that filled the skies and blotted out the night, of the thirst and the hunger and the screaming of those dying, of the invisible poisons that permeated the air and plants and waters of the world. And most of all, he spoke of the deaths of men, children, and women, and of the deaths of beasts, and when I listened, I wept with him, though

I did not know if he had imagined it all or if he was somehow really able to remember something he had not seen firsthand.

According to the orthodox history of the Great White, only the righteous were spared. But Maruman said those spared had the luck of living a long way from the center of destruction and that was all. If he was right, then all that the Herders had told us were lies, and the Council, supposedly devised by Lud, was more likely man-made, too.

It was then I had begun to understand what my parents had been fighting for with more than blind loyalty.

Maruman bit me, bored with my musings; then he licked the place as demanded by courtesy. I looked fondly at him, wondering where his wandering had taken him this time.

"Where have you been? I missed you," I told him.

He purred. "I am here now," he answered firmly, and I knew better than to question him further. He did not like to be questioned, and when he did not want to talk, the worst course was to press him. Gradually, over time, he would give me enough information to work out the rest, but for now I noticed a few places where his fur had rubbed off and assumed he had been to tainted land. If that was true, he would almost certainly undergo another of his mad periods. I resolved to feed him up, because he did not eat at such times and was already too thin.

"She is coming," he sent suddenly, and looking at his eyes, I saw that he was already half into a fey state, and his words were probably only raving.

Nonetheless, I asked, "Who is coming?"

"She. The darkOne," he answered. "She seeks you

but does not know you." A thrill of fear coursed through me. His thoughts seemed to tally with my own persistent visions of being sought. "She comes soon. The whiteface smells of her." Maruman spat at the moon, which had risen in the daytime sky. It was full. I wondered why he hated the moon so much. It had something to do with the coming of the Great White, I knew.

He snapped at nothing above his injured ear, then yowled forlornly.

"When does she come?" I asked, but Maruman seemed to have lost the thread of the conversation. I watched his mind drift into his eyes. He growled and the hackles on his back rose, then he shook his head as if to clear it of the fog that sometimes floated there.

"When I was on the dreamtrails, I met the oldOne. She said I must follow you. It is my task. But I am . . . tired."

"Follow me where?" I asked. Then I gulped, for a horrible notion had come to me. "Where does the dark-One come from? Where will she take me?"

"To the mountains," Maruman answered. "To the mountains of shadow, where black wars with white, to the heart of darkness, to the aerie above the clouds, to the chasm underearth. To the others." Suddenly he pitched sideways, and a trickle of saliva came from his mouth.

I sat very still, because none lived in the mountains save those at Obernewtyn.

A keeper from Obernewtyn would come; if Maruman was right, it would be a woman who would find out the truth about me.

✦ *4* ✦

Like every child, I had heard stories about Obernewtyn. Parents and orphanage guardians used it as a sort of horror tale to make naughty children behave. But, in truth, very little was known about it.

In its early days, the Council had been approached by Lukas Seraphim, who had built a huge holding in the wilds of the northern mountains, on land ringed by savage peaks and only just free of the Blacklands. He had offered this holding as a solution to the problem of where to send the worst-afflicted Misfits and those who were too troublesome for use on the Councilfarms.

In the end, an agreement had been made to send some Misfits to Obernewtyn, where they would be put to work. A few generations later, the agreement still stood. Some said it was just like another Councilfarm and that the master there only sought labor for an area too remote to interest normal laborers. Others said the Seraphim family was itself afflicted in some way and pitied the creatures, while still others claimed they practiced the dark arts and needed human subjects.

Those Misfits taken there were never seen again, so none of these stories had ever been authenticated properly. But such was the legend of Obernewtyn, grown over the years because of its very mystery, and it was feared by all orphans, not the least because in more modern times, it sent out its keepers to investigate the homes, seeking undisclosed Misfits among us.

It was said these keepers were extraordinarily skillful at spotting aberrations, and that the resultant Council trial was a foregone conclusion.

If what I feared was true, Maruman's garbled predictions and my own premonitions could only add up to a visit by a keeper from Obernewtyn. In the past, I had been fortunate enough never to have been present at a home under such review, but it was an occasion I had dreaded, particularly as my abilities made me far more deviant than any Misfit I had ever heard of.

When official word of an Obernewtyn keeper's imminent arrival was circulated, my worst fears were realized. All the omens implied disaster.

Jes was worried enough to catch me alone in the garden and advise me to be careful. His warning itself did not surprise me, but he looked scared, and that made him more approachable. Impulsively, I told him of my premonition, but that only made him angry. "Don't start that business now," he said.

"I'm afraid," I said in a small voice.

His eyes softened, and to my surprise, he took one of my hands and squeezed it reassuringly. "She can't possibly know what you are unless she is like you." I stared because that was the first time in many years he had mentioned my secret without bitterness.

He went on. "Look, why do you think everyone finds out she's coming before she gets here? They do it deliberately, to scare people. If people are nervous, they're more likely to give themselves away."

Wanting badly to please him, I nodded in agreement.

He looked surprised and rather pleased; we had done nothing but argue for a long time.

We smiled at each other hesitantly.

The keeper arrived three days later, and by then, the atmosphere in the home was electric. Even the guardians were jumpy, and the Herders' lectures had grown longer and more dogmatic. A keeper could not have wished for more.

Like me, many of the orphans had never seen an Obernewtyn keeper. I was amazed to see how beautiful she was, and not at all threatening. It was impossible to look at her petite, fashionably attired form and credit the Gothic horror stories that abounded in connection with Obernewtyn.

She was introduced to us at a special assembly as Madam Vega, head keeper of Obernewtyn.

The orphans who met her spoke of her beauty and sweetness and gentle manner. Nothing was as we had imagined, and nothing happened in those few days to cast any suspicion on me. I was even able to convince myself that both Maruman and I must have been mistaken. Even so, I greeted the morning of her departure with a kind of relief.

I was working in the kitchen when one of the guardians instructed me to prepare a tea tray for the Kinraide head and her guest. It was an innocent enough request, but as I wheeled the laden tray to the front interviewing chamber, I felt uneasy. I took a deep breath to calm myself.

The head was standing near the door when I entered and gestured impatiently for me to transfer the tea things from my tray to a low table. I did this rather awkwardly, wondering where Madam Vega was. I reached out with my abilities to locate her, an act that always made me feel oddly exposed because it required me to unshield my mind. Sensing that she was at the other end of the room, I turned to see her standing at the purple-draped window, her back to the room as she looked out over Kinraide's broad formal gardens.

Then, slowly, she turned around.

When she turned, it seemed she went on turning for an eternity, gradually showing more of herself. Struck with the dreadful curiosity of fear, unable to look away, I became convinced that when her movement was completed eons from now, I would be looking into the face of my most terrible nightmares.

Yet she was smiling at me, and her eyes were blue like the summer sky. She hastened to where I stood.

I swallowed, too scared to move until the Kinraide head gestured for me to pour the tea. My hands shook.

"My dear child," said Madam Vega, taking the teapot from me with her own lovely white hands, "you're trembling." Then she turned to the head with a faint look of reproach.

"She has been ill," the other woman said with a shrug. I prayed she would dismiss me, but she was sugaring her tea.

The keeper looked at me. "You seem upset. Now, why would that be, I wonder? Are you afraid?"

I shook my head, but of course she did not believe me.

"You need not fear me. I'm aware of all the silly stories. How they began, I really don't know. I am simply here to take away those children who are afflicted with mental problems. Obernewtyn is a beautiful place—

though cold, I admit," she added confidingly. "But there is nothing there to frighten anyone. And my good master seeks only to find a cure for such afflictions. He thinks it is possible to do this before the mind is full grown."

"A noble purpose," murmured the other woman piously.

Madam Vega had been watching me very closely as she spoke. I felt as if I were drowning in the extraordinary blueness of her eyes. There was something almost hypnotic in them.

"I know a great deal about Misfits," she said.

I wanted to look away but couldn't, and an urge grew within me to find out what she was thinking. I let the edge of my shield fade.

In an instant, a dozen impressions pierced me like blades, but beneath the blue compulsion of her eyes, they faded.

"Well, well," she said, and stepped away from me.

I stood for a moment, half dazed.

"Well, go along, then," said the Kinraide head impatiently.

I turned on shaking legs, willing myself not to run. As I closed the door behind me, I heard Madam Vega's sweet voice utter the words that spelled my doom. "What did you say that girl was called?"

· 5 ·

"Jes!" I stumbled into the kitchen, sending out a cloud of panic and urgency. "Jes. Jes. Jes!"

I almost fell over the astonished Rosamunde, who was working there. "Elspeth?" she said disbelievingly.

Jes charged through another door, his face contorted with fury. "What are you doing?" he shouted. Noticing Rosamunde, he stopped to stare at us in confusion.

"For Lud's sake, Jes, don't yell at her. It's one of her fainting fits again." Rosamunde looked uncertainly at me. "That water must have been tainted, despite what the Herder said."

"Water?" Jes whispered incredulously.

"Of course," she said sternly. "And stop glaring at her. She's just been in with the Obernewtyn keeper. I'll get a powder," she added, and departed.

"Is it true?" he asked, fear in his eyes.

I nodded numbly. "I was only meant to serve tea. But she knows now."

"How can you be sure?" he pressed. "Tell me what they said. Did they speak of me?"

"They said nothing. But at the end, when I was leaving, she asked who I was."

He gaped. "That's all?"

I shook my head. "She knows, Jes."

The light died in his eyes. He might despise my powers, but he did not doubt them.

"Jes!" It was Rosamunde. She frowned at him from the veranda. "Don't stare her down like some idiot guardian. Help her outside. Some fresh air will revive her."

"She's all right," Jes snapped, but he carried me onto the veranda and set me on a couch. Ignoring him, Rosamunde handed me a powder. I swallowed it without demur, hardly noticing its bitter aftertaste.

"I am sorry," I told Jes, suddenly remorseful.

He made no reply. His face was grim. I could not blame his hatred of my abilities. At that moment, I hated them myself.

Rosamunde had noticed the look on Jes's face and sat on the couch beside him. "What is the matter? Tell me. You know you can trust me. I'll help if I can."

He looked at her, and to my astonishment, I could see that he did trust her. Lying to this girl would not come easily to him. I studied her properly. She was a plain, sensitive-looking girl, pale as most orphans were, with a mop of brown curls neatly tied back. I wondered how I had been so blind as to miss the thawing of my self-sufficient brother.

Jes turned to face me. "Are you all right, Elf?" he asked. That had been his pet name for me in happier days, but he had not used it for a long time. How odd that it had taken a disaster to show me that there was still some bond of affection between us. His face was thoughtful, and as I had often done before, I wished I could read his mind. He was not like me, yet his was one of the rare minds that seemed to have a natural shield.

Rosamunde gazed at us both in consternation. "Tell me, please," she urged.

"Elspeth will be declared a Misfit," Jes said tiredly.

"You poor thing," Rosamunde whispered.

"Elf . . . has begun to have unnatural dreams," Jes said slowly.

I stared at him. Occasionally I had true-dreamed, but that was the least of it. Why was Jes lying?

"It was the tainted water," Jes continued, his eyes evasive.

I gaped openly now.

"But . . . everyone knows that sometimes happens when someone comes into contact with tainted water," Rosamunde said incredulously. "She was normal before the accident, and I am sure that will temper their judgment. She might only go to the Councilfarms, and you could petition for her once you have your own Normalcy Certificate."

Then a look of concern passed over her features, and I knew what had occurred to her. If I was declared a birth Misfit, Jes would be stripped of his armband and privileges, and even his Certificate would be in doubt. On the other hand, if the Council judged that I had been affected by tainted water and declared me Misfit through misadventure, Jes's status would be unaffected.

I looked at my brother. I had never known what motivated him. But perhaps he thought of more than just himself as he weaved this tissue of lies. After all, it would go easier for me, too, if the Council thought I was a Misfit only by accident.

"Talk to them," Rosamunde urged Jes, but he shook his head. "You are no Misfit!" she cried.

"No," Jes agreed. His eyes were sad. "Leave us," he said to Rosamunde gently.

She burst into noisy tears. "No. I will come, too, if they take you. I could pretend—"

"Be wise," Jes said. "We don't know what the keeper will do, or what happens at Obernewtyn." He paused, and I sensed the struggle taking place within him. "If things had been different . . . ," he began, and then stopped. He fell silent, his face troubled.

Rosamunde seemed to understand and dried her tears. Her face was wretched with unhappiness. "They might not take you," she said. "The tainted water is to blame."

I looked at her, and a plan came to me. I would have to be wary and delicate.

Carefully I directed my ability to manipulate thoughts into her reeling mind, seeking to create the chains of thought and action I needed, joining them carefully onto her own half-formed notions. I had not used my coercing ability so directly before, and I was curious to see how well the thoughts and decisions I had grafted would hold.

"You must go," Jes told her. "I want you to go. Never speak of this—or us—again. It is bad enough that we have been seen together. I will not let you be dragged into this mess."

"Oh Lud, no," she sobbed, and ran inside.

Jes and I looked at each other, neither of us having the slightest idea what the other thought.

"Elspeth Gordie."

I trembled at the sound of my name, though I had been waiting for it. At that last moment, there was a flare of hope that I had been wrong after all.

I waited, still trembling, as those around me drew

39

back. The head of Kinraide went on to say that I had been affected by tainted water and was to be sent to the Councilcourt in Sutrium for sentencing. I knew then my plan had worked. I looked at Jes and caught his amazed look. He did not understand how the lie he had devised had come to be believed by the guardians. I prayed I knew him well enough to guess he would not protest or ask who had reported me. My eyes sought out Rosamunde, who would not look at me, and I hoped she would not be too badly affected by what I had willed her to do. I felt a self-loathing for having burdened her with a betrayal she would never have contemplated without my coercerthought.

Her denouncement had come too late to stop the proceedings under which I would be bonded to Obernewtyn, but it had saved Jes from any trouble and had categorized me as a very ordinary sort of Misfit. I prayed the knowledge that she had saved Jes would be enough to salve Rosamunde. I did not want her to suffer.

An awful lethargy filled me as I sat in the punishment room, where I would remain until the Council coach came for me at dawn. I could have picked the lock, for I had recently discovered that by concentrating fiercely I could exert a small amount of physical force with my mental powers. But were I to open the door, where would I go?

Maruman came to my prison window that night. I tried to explain that I was going away, but he was still under the sway of his fit, and I could not tell how much he understood.

"The mountains have called at last," he said dreamily.

"Last night I dreamed of the oldOne again. She said your destiny is there."

"Oh, don't," I begged, but Maruman was merciless in his fey state.

"I smell the white in the mountains," he told me with drifting eyes that reflected the moonlight. I found myself trembling after he had gone and wished that now, of all times, Maruman had been his grumpy, sensible self, all too ready to scoff at my fears.

I slept fitfully until I heard movement at the door. It was still not dawn, and I wondered if the carriage had arrived already. But it was Jes.

"Forgive me," he said.

I gaped at him.

"I didn't tell them that business about the water. I swear. I . . . I thought of it, to save myself, but I didn't. I don't know how they came to know. I wouldn't blame you for thinking I had done it," he said wretchedly.

"It's better that they think I am only a dreamer and not a birth Misfit," I said earnestly, hoping he would not confess his anguish to poor Rosamunde, who might reveal her part in my denunciation.

"It shames me that when they read your name out I thought only of myself," he said in a muffled voice.

He seemed to feel he had betrayed me simply because the thought had occurred to him, and I sensed his rigid nature would crumble completely if I allowed him to break down.

"Soon you will have your Certificate. You will be able to petition for me," I said softly.

"But Obernewtyn does not release those it takes," he whispered.

Hastily I took his hand. "Oh, Jes," I said. "You saw the keeper. Did she look so awful? I'm not frightened. And I would have hated the Councilfarms," I added with a smile.

Wanly he smiled back.

There was a movement outside, and a voice called that the carriage was ready. I looked at Jes in sudden concern, fearing what would happen if he was caught with me. But seeing my alarm, he shook his head, saying the Herder himself had given permission for Jes to say prayers for my soul. I noticed he still wore the armband, but I said nothing.

He leaned forward suddenly, his eyes fierce. "I will come and get you one day. I promise."

But you are only sixteen, I thought, *with two more long years until you can apply for your Certificate.* Instinct told me this would be our last goodbye. Impulsively, I flung my arms around him. "Dear Jes, it really is best this way," I said. "Except for our parting, I am honestly glad it is done with."

"Time now," said the guardian. Jes nodded. Suddenly aware that he was being watched, he said the last few chants of a prayer.

"Goodbye," I whispered.

He did not wait to see me bundled into the dark coach, and I was glad for it.

I sat back into the stiff upholstery and wondered what destiny waited for me at Obernewtyn.

✦ 6 ✦

THERE WERE FEW people around to see me arrive at the Councilcourt in Sutrium. Even at the busiest hour, few tarried near those somber buildings. The white slate steps led up to the open double doors, and for the second time in my life, I ascended them, led by a soldierguard. The smell of wood polish made me vividly recollect my last visit. But back then, Jes had been with me, squeezing my hand.

"Sit and wait till you are called," said the soldierguard, peering into my face as if to ascertain whether I was capable of understanding. I nodded dully, and he went away.

A man and a boy came through the front door. There was something unusual about them, but I felt too numb at first to try working out what it was. Then it came to me. They were very tanned, as if they had spent their whole life outdoors.

The man followed a soldierguard through a door, while the boy looked around to find I was sitting on the only bench. He sat beside me.

"Hullo," he said.

I stared at him, astonished that he would speak to a complete stranger. And here of all places. "Who are you?" I asked, suddenly suspicious.

He looked amused, and his eyes crinkled in a nice sort of way. "Do I look like a spy?" he laughed. "My name is Daffyd. My uncle is petitioning the council for a permit to trade in the mountains."

"The mountains," I echoed.

"Well, not exactly the mountains. After all, whom would we trade with? I meant the high country," he explained. He smiled again, and despite everything, I found myself smiling back. "Why are you here?" he asked.

"I'm a Misfit, or soon to be judged so," I said bluntly. "I am to be sent to Obernewtyn."

He didn't recoil. He only said, "Well, if you are like me, you will find the mountains beautiful. I don't have much patience for places like Sutrium," he added disparagingly.

Impulsively I tried to read him, but like Jes, he had a natural shield.

"Aren't you afraid to be seen talking to a Misfit?" I asked at last.

"Where I come from, they say Misfits are people who have been punished by Lud. I don't see how that is anything to fear. In truth it seems to me there are worse things than being a Misfit."

"Oh yes?" I asked sarcastically. "What could be worse?"

"These people, for one. This Luddamned Council," he said in a low, intense voice. I stared, for what he was saying was sedition. He was either mad or insanely careless.

Seeing my expression, he only shrugged. "These fools believe everyone who doesn't think and act as they do is evil. As for Obernewtyn, you need not fear it.

It is merely a large mansion with farms. Not those labor camps the Council calls a farm. Real farms, with animals and crops and sowing and reaping. You might like it," he said reassuringly.

"Have you been there?" I asked.

His eyes were suddenly evasive, and though I did not press him, his unexpected reluctance angered me. "I might escape," I told him coldly, more for effect than because I meant it.

But he gave me a measured look. "If ever you do run away, you might seek out the Druid in the highlands. I have heard he lives still in hiding. He has no love for Misfits, but you need not tell him—"

He broke off his words at the sound of footsteps, and we both looked up to see his uncle reenter the room. "Come, Daffyd," the older man said, his eyes skidding over me.

Daffyd rose at once. He said nothing to me, but as they moved to the door, he smiled over his shoulder.

I watched them go thoughtfully. Henry Druid had been a Herder, forced to flee with some of his followers after defying a Council directive to burn his precious collection of Oldtime books. That had been long years past, and rumor was that he had died. Yet this boy implied otherwise.

I shrugged. The boy had surely been defective. He had been careless in talking to me at all.

A soldierguard stepped from one of the doors and waved impatiently for me to enter. I went slowly, playing the part of a dull wit.

The trial room was quite small. At the very front was a Councilman seated at a high bench, facing the rest of the room. Beside him at a lower table were two Herders.

The rows of seats facing the front were occupied only by a few lounging soldierguards in their telltale yellow cloaks. The seats were theoretically meant for interested members of the community, but I could not imagine anyone would be curious enough to risk being associated with whoever was on trial. No one paid the slightest bit of attention as I was prodded to the front by the soldierguard on duty. I looked up at the Councilman, wondering bitterly what would happen to the daughter of such a person if *she* were judged Misfit.

"Well, now," said the Councilman in a brisk voice. His eyes passed over me with disinterest, reminding me that I was less than nothing to him. "I understand this is a routine affair with no defense," he said to a tall man in black who rose and nodded languidly.

The Councilman turned his attention to me. "You are Elspeth Gordie?"

I nodded.

"Very well. You have been accused of being a Misfit by Madam Vega of Obernewtyn. If so judged, you will be unfit ever to receive a Normalcy Certificate or to become part of the community of true humans. Corsak, you will speak for Stephen Seraphim, the Master of Obernewtyn?"

The man in black did not look at me as he spoke. "This orphan has been exposed as a Misfit by the Obernewtyn head keeper. She was also denounced by another orphan, who claims that she fell in tainted water and has from that time had unnatural dreams and fainting fits. This would normally mark her a Misfit by mischance, but there are several other points. May I expand?"

The Councilman nodded.

"In her first home, the girl was accused of giving an evil eye. Naturally we do not place too much credibility on these reports, but they do point to the possibility that she had Misfit tendencies even before this tainted water infected her." As he continued outlining various reports made about me in various homes, both by other orphans and by guardians, I began to feel truly frightened. I had never imagined my record would hold so much evidence to suggest I was a birth Misfit. It was suddenly clear to me that I would never have been issued a Normalcy Certificate.

Suddenly the Councilman cut him off. "I do not see how any of this gossip is as significant as the fact that the girl came into contact with tainted water. Surely that is the cause of any mutancy. And is it not still true that your master has no interest in those made Misfit by mischance?"

"That is so, Councilman," Corsak said carefully. "But that evidence was not available at the time Madam Vega made her initial claim."

"And your master. Does he still feel there is some hope of a cure for Misfits?"

"Obernewtyn concentrates all its efforts on healing," the man in black answered somewhat defensively.

One of the Herders stood. "Misfits are not sick. They have allowed themselves to become habitations for demons."

Sirrah Corsak bowed. "My master feels it is the sickness that allows the invasion of demons, and that a young mind might be healed so that the demons could be driven out."

The Herder glanced at his companion, an older priest who also rose. He wore a gold-edged armband

47

that denoted him the senior of the pair. "Driving away demons is Herder work," he said.

"Of course," said the Obernewtyn representative. "If a mind were to be healed, the subject would immediately be delivered to the Herder Faction."

"Yet where are your successes, Sirrah Corsak?" asked the first Herder aggressively. "Why should we keep sending Misfits to you, when none are healed?"

The Obernewtyn man cast an appealing look at the Councilman. "You are well paid for them," he said.

"That is not the point," snapped the Councilman. He nodded at the two Herders, who again sat down.

The man in black looked nervous. "I beg pardon, Councilman," he said. "It is true that Obernewtyn uses these Misfits for labor, but my master diligently seeks a cure as well."

The Councilman eyed him coolly. "So you have said, and so Madam Vega and your master have scribed. Even so, perhaps it is time for us to visit Obernewtyn and evaluate for ourselves what is done with the Misfits we send there."

His eyes flicked back to me. "Do you admit to being a Misfit?" he asked in a bored tone.

I cringed and gave him what I hoped was a convincingly vacant leer. The Councilman sighed as if it were as much as he had expected, then asked if anyone knew whether I was able to speak. No one answered, and the Councilman scowled impatiently.

"Very well, I pronounce her Misfit by mischance. But you may take her, Corsak. Make arrangements to name her in the records when you make the bond over. And we look forward to an invitation to visit Obernewtyn and to see these healing efforts you have described with such eloquence," he added meaningfully.

Corsak nodded and indicated for me to follow him.

The Councilman forestalled him coldly. "If you please. Is the scribe here?"

"Yes!" said a cheerful voice.

"Ensure this reaches the people. Misfits are a particularly foul and insidious threat to our community. They often pass as normal for many years, since their defects are not obvious to the eye. We know this because of the efforts of our good and diligent Herders." The two Herders inclined their heads modestly. "They have lately informed me that their researches have revealed that Misfits are Lud's way of punishing our laxity. How is it, Lud asks us, that Misfits are permitted to roam and breed among us for so long? The answer is that we have failed in our duty of watchfulness. This attitude threatens to hurl us back into the Age of Chaos, and worse. Therefore, it is the order and decree of this Councilcourt that penalties for aiding and concealing Misfits and any other defective humans or beasts will increase. Each man must watch his neighbor. . . ."

He went on to explain the various new rulings and penalties, and I shuddered at the effect this would have on the community. Each time the Council sought to tighten its control, a new wave of denunciations and burnings occurred. Oddly enough, I fancied a look of surprise had crossed the face of the younger priest at the mention of Herder researches.

◆ 7 ◆

IT TOOK SOME time to reach the outskirts of Sutrium. I
had forgotten the city was so big. The streets were completely deserted, and it was well into the morning before we reached the end of the town's sprawling outer
limits, but toward midday, the city fell rapidly behind.

I had lived in urban orphan homes now for many
years, but the curved road parting the soft folded hills
and gullies brought back clear memories of my childhood in Rangorn, far from the towns and the ever-
present menace of the Council. I realized I had not lied
to Jes when I told him I was almost glad. There was an
odd sort of peace in having got the thing done at last. I
thought of Madam Vega and reflected that Obernewtyn
was bound to be less terrible than the stories.

It was not hard to forget fear and to surrender myself to the peaceful solitude of the carriage. The morning burgeoned into a sun-filled day, and between naps I
watched the country unfold.

To the east of the road, we passed the villages of
Saithwold and Sawlney, and beyond them to the north
were soft woodlands, where from the window I could
see the downs sloping gently to Arandelft, set deep in
the forest. To the west of the road were the vast hazy
moors of Glenelg.

The road curved down to pass on the farthermost outskirts of Arandelft, where slate-gray buildings were framed by cultivated fields flanked by bloodberry trees. More than twenty leagues away and closing the horizon was the Gelfort Range—the mountains Tor, Aren Craggie, and Emeralfel. They marked the border of the highlands, and as if to underline this, the road began gradually to incline upward.

We passed onto the low westernmost slopes of the Brown Haw Rises, hillocky and undulant—I was astounded to discover how much I knew of land I had never seen. My father had talked a good deal of these places. He had traveled much in the Land before he bonded with my mother. Sometimes he had seated me on his knee and shown me colored pictures that he called maps. He would point to places, tell me their names, and explain what they were like.

We passed a small moor, wetter and more dense than Glenelg, and I peered through the leafy eben trees along the roadside at the mist-wreathed expanse. There had been no moors in Rangorn, but I recognized this from my father's descriptions. He had said the mists never went away but were always fed by some hissing subterranean source. He thought the moors were caused by some inner disturbance in the earth, yet another legacy of the Great White.

My mother had said good herbs always grew near the moors; she came from the high country and knew a great deal about herb lore. I thought of the great, white-trunked trees that had stood on the hillside around our house. Were they still there, though the house had long ago been reduced to ashes? I remembered my mother making me listen to the whispering sounds of the trees;

51

the rich, shadowed glades where we collected mushrooms and healing flowers; and the summer brambles laden with fat berries, dragging over the bank of our favorite swimming hole. I thought of standing with my father and looking down from the hills to where the Ford of Rangorn met the onrush of the Suggredoon, and the distant, grayish glint of a Blacklands lake.

And I remembered the burning of my mother and father, in the midst of all the beauty of Rangorn. Perhaps that was what Jes remembered most, what had made him so cold and strange in recent times.

As the late-afternoon sun slanted through the window of the carriage, we halted briefly at a wayside hostel, and a new coachman came to take the place of the other. The hostel was just outside a village called Guanette, and I felt a jolt at the name. It made me think of Maruman, and I wondered if he had understood that I really was going away for good.

We rode on, and I saw that the village consisted mostly of small stone-wrought hovels with shingled roofs. They looked ancient and had probably been erected during the Age of Chaos. Their stolidity seemed a response to the turmoiled past.

Laughter drifted in through the windows as we rode by children who scrabbled in pools of dust along the roadway. They looked up indifferently as we passed. I was once like them, I thought rather bitterly, until the Council had taken a hand.

The carriage jerked suddenly to a halt, and the coachman dismounted. We had stopped outside yet another hostel called The Green Tree.

After a long time, he came back, unlocked a window, and threw a soft parcel to me. "Supper," he grunted in a curious accent. Impulsively, I asked him if I could sit outside and eat.

He hesitated, then unlocked the door. "Out yer get, then," he said.

Thanking him profusely, I did as he bade, and he re-locked the carriage, muttering about children. I stood blinking at him. "Go round th' back. Ye can eat there. Mind ye don't wander." Thanking him again, I hastened away, thinking many of the late-night callers at my father's house had spoken like this, with a slow, singsong lilt. They had looked like this man, too, gnarled and brown with kind eyes.

There was a pretty, unkempt garden out behind the hostel, and I scoured it for a spot under one of the trees.

"Least you/Elspeth could do is share food/meal," came a plaintive thought. I jumped to my feet in fright, dropping the food parcel. Maruman rushed forward and sniffed it tenderly. "Now look what you have done."

I stared at him, unable to believe my eyes. "What . . . how did you get here?" Maruman gave me a sly cat-look and fell to tearing at the parcel. I sat back, my own appetite forgotten.

"I came with you," he told me as he ate. "In the box with wheels, on the back. I am very clever," he added smugly.

I burst out laughing; then I looked around in fright, because my laughter had sounded so loud.

"You took a terrible risk," I sent. "What if you had been seen?"

"I had to come/follow," he sent. "Innle must be protected."

I looked into his eyes, but there was no sign of

53

madness. "You won't be able to come all the way to Obernewtyn," I sent. "The carriage goes over tainted ground."

"I will stay here, and you will come to me."

I shook my head impatiently. "Obernewtyn is like a cage. I won't be allowed to do as I please."

Unperturbed, Maruman began cleaning one of his paws. "You will come," he sent at last. "Maruman does not like the mountains. I smell the white there."

"Well, how will you live here?" I asked him.

He gave me a scornful look; Maruman had, after all, lived a good many years before meeting me. Just the same, I reflected, he was not a young cat, and then there were his fits of madness. Finishing his ablutions, he curled in my lap and went to sleep.

I thought of what I had said to Daffyd, the boy in the Councilcourt. I had not meant it then, but now I seriously considered escaping. I could run off; it would be far easier here than it would have been in Sutrium. I could find work in some remote hamlet and keep Maruman with me. The thought of escape made me feel breathless.

My mother once had bought a wild bird from an old man who caught the poor things. We hadn't much money, but she had a soft heart. He had given her the oldest bird, an ugly creature he had had for some time. She had opened the cage to let it fly away. But it was a poor half-starved thing and would not go even when prodded. It died there, huddled in the corner of the cage. My mother had said it had been caged for too long. Neither Jes nor I had understood then, but I wondered if, like that bird, I had been caged too long to contemplate freedom.

A voice called my name. Maruman woke immediately. He leapt from my knee and melted into the shadows just as the coachman and a woman came onto the porch of the hostel. The old man blinked, and I sensed he had seen Maruman, but he said nothing. The woman turned to him. "Just as well for you that she did not wander away." She flicked her hand at me. "Get into the carriage."

I followed them to the road with an inward sigh, noticing the horses had been changed. The woman climbed heavily into the seat and glared at me as she settled herself.

"I am Guardian Hester," she said.

I waited, but she seemed to feel it was beneath her to say more. She yawned several times and soon seemed bored. Eventually she took a small vial from her pocket, uncorked it, and drank the contents. I recognized the bitter odor of the sleep drug. In a short time, she was dozing.

After leaving Guanette, the country grew steadily steeper. The road was still well cobbled, but it became progressively more narrow and winding. The coachman maneuvered carefully around the bends, for on one side was a sharp drop to a darkly wooded valley extending as far as the eye could see. It was slow going, and after about an hour, he pulled the coach over to the right of the road to fetch the horses water from a spring. I called out to him.

"Hey," he grumbled as he came to the window and peered in at me. "Is that my name, then?"

"I'm sorry. No one tells us names. Can I ride up there with you?"

Predictably he shook his head, peering in at the

guardian's sleeping form. "If ye were alone, maybe I would let ye," he said softly. "But if she were to waken an' see ye gone . . ." He shook his head in anticipation of the coals of wrath that would be heaped on his head.

"But she won't wake for hours. She took some of that sleep stuff." I poked her hard to show him I spoke the truth.

He ruminated for a moment, then took out his keys.

"Oh, thank you," I gasped, astounded at my luck.

"Well fine of me it is," he agreed. "But she better not wake, or I'll be in deep troubles." He finished watering the horses while I capered in the crisp highland air. "Enoch," the coachman said suddenly.

"Pardon?" I said.

"Enoch, girl," he repeated. "That's my name." He helped me up onto the seat beside him, and I felt a thrill as he clicked his tongue and the coach began to move.

"My name . . . ," I began to say, then stopped. Perhaps he wouldn't want to know my name. Misfits, after all, weren't supposed to be quite human.

"Your name?" he prompted; encouraged, I told him. He nodded and then pointed to the valley to the west. "That's the White Valley."

I stared, thinking that Maruman would not like the name. Enoch went on. "Many have gone to that valley in search of refuge, but it ain't a friendly place. Strange animals rove there, an' they don't love men."

"Maybe that's where Henry Druid perished," I said, to see how he would respond.

The old man gave me a sharp look. "Accordin' to yon Council, he died in the highlands, true enow, an' some say they have seen his ghost walk. Me, I dinna

56

believe in ghosts." He saw my quick look of interest, and his expression went bland.

I looked at the wood and wondered whether the Druid still lived.

"That were a fine cat," the coachman said presently. "Some don't like cats. Reckon they're incapable of love or loyalty, but I dinna agree. A cat can love, fierce as any beast."

"He's not a very pretty cat," I said hesitantly.

The old man grinned. "All that's fine is nowt necessarily fair. Look at me. But as a matter of fact, I thought that cat a handsome creature." He glanced at me. "I've a good mind to have a bit of a look for him. Maybe he'd fancy living with me. Of course, he might not take to me."

"Oh, he will!" I cried. "I am sure of it."

The coachman grinned and nodded, and we rode for some distance in companionable silence. Perhaps Enoch would find Maruman. I hoped so.

The valley was lost to sight at last as we wound into the mountains. "That stuff would kill a pig," said the coachman. He jerked his head back to where the guardian slept. "Now, me mam gave us herbs when we couldn't sleep. Good natural things. That were good enough for us."

"But herb lore is banned," I said.

He looked taken aback. "An' so it is. Damned if I didn't forget fer a minute. But it weren't so when I were a lad." He paused, seemingly struck by the oddness of something that had been a good thing in his youth but which had since become evil in the eyes of the community. Finally, he sighed as if the problem were unresolvable. "Things were different then," he said.

Looking around, he pointed again to where we had come back into the open. The mountains hid the White Valley from us, but there was a broad plain on the other side of the road. "Th' land hereabout is Darthnor, and th' village of Darthnor is that way," Enoch said, nodding to the east. I stared but could see no sign of any settlement. " 'Tis a strange place," he said, "an' I say so even though I were born there. None dwell in these parts but a few shepherds. Those in the village are mostly miners, but I reckon th' ground here is tainted, so I dinna go under it as me father did before me." He looked sad. Then his expression sharpened and he brought the coach to a halt.

"Ye'll have to get in now. Soon we come to tainted ground, an' the vapors are pure poison," he said.

Regretfully I climbed down and held the horses while the coachman tied rags around their noses and faces, and bags on their hooves.

"Won't you get sick?" I asked. He shook his head, saying that he would be all right for the short time we would be on tainted earth. Nonetheless, he tied a scarf around his face before leading me back to the carriage.

Suddenly he gave a shout and pointed up. I looked but saw nothing.

"That were a Guanette bird," he explained. "Ye missed it, an' that's a shame, for 'tis a rare sight."

"A Guanette bird?" I gaped, thinking I had misheard him. "I thought they were extinct."

Enoch shook his head. "Nowt extinct, but I guess it might be better to be thought so. They're rare, and rare things are hunted. That village back there were named after them by the first Master of Obernewtyn, Sirrah Lukas Seraphim. A grand queer man he must have been to make his home up there with the Blacklands all round. His grandson is master up there now."

There was a subtly different note in his voice at the mention of the present Master of Obernewtyn.

"Have you seen him?" I asked, hoping to elicit further information.

"He never comes down from the mountains," said the coachman. A strange look crossed his face, but it was so brief I thought I had imagined it.

"In ye go," he said. I clambered into the carriage. On the verge of locking the door again, Enoch hesitated. "Look, if ye be special fond of animals, I've a friend of sorts up there. His name be Rushton. Tell him I vouch for ye, an' maybe he'll find a job ye'll like."

But before I could thank him, he had locked me in, and the carriage lurched as he resumed his seat.

✦ 8 ✦

I DREAMED.

In my dream, I was somewhere cold and darkly quiet. I could hear water dripping, and I was afraid, though I didn't know why. I seemed to be waiting for something.

In the distance, there was a bright flash of light. A feeling of urgency made me hasten toward the light, stumbling over uneven ground I could not see. A high-pitched whining noise filled the air like a scream, but no one could scream for so long without stopping to breathe. I sensed danger, but the compulsion to find the light overrode my instincts. Again it flashed, apparently no closer than before. I could not tell what the source was, though it was obviously unnatural.

All at once, a voice spoke inside me. Shocked, I skidded to a halt, for it was a human voice.

"Tell me," the voice said. "Tell me."

There was a sharp pain behind my eyes, and I flinched in astonishment that a voice could hurt me, understanding at the same time that the whining noise and the voice inside me were connected. I turned to run, at last obeying the urge to escape. Then the ground beneath me burst into flames, and I screamed.

I woke and stared wildly about, my heart thundering even as the nightmare faded. I could feel perspiration on my hands and back. I lay there trying to think what such a dream might mean. I rarely dreamed so intensely.

It was dark, and bruised purple clouds scudded across the sky. A distant cracking noise heralded the coming storm, and within moments, a flash of lightning illuminated the barren landscape. There was a rumble of thunder, then another crack, and this time the scent of charred wood drifted in through the window. I pitied Enoch and hoped Maruman was somewhere safe.

I sensed the unease of the animals, and with each crash of thunder, their tension grew; yet I had the odd impression it was not the storm but something else that unnerved them. There was another loud crash, very close, and a log fell right alongside the carriage.

The horses' suppressed terror erupted, and they bolted, plunging along the road at a mad pace, jerking the coach after them like some doomed creature being dragged to its death. I could hear Enoch's blasphemous thoughts as he fought to control the maddened team.

Clinging to my seat, I looked down at the guardian, who continued to sleep. Branches scraped at the window; the road had suddenly narrowed, and we were in the midst of a thick clump of gnarled trees. I hoped none would fall, for they were big enough to crush the carriage.

A blinding gray rain fell as we passed from the trees and out into the open again. I could see very little because of the rain and the darkness, but the landscape looked barren and ugly. Then the rain stopped as abruptly as a tap turned off.

The silence that followed was so complete it was uncanny. The horses were under control again, and I heard a tired snort from one. The sound almost echoed in the stillness. It had grown fractionally lighter, and I could see sparse trees drooping wearily. I thought the land must indeed be cursed for the fury of nature to strike at it so mercilessly.

Then, before my eyes, the land seemed to transform itself from a barren place to the bleakest, deadest piece of earth. It was impossible to imagine a single blade of grass or even the most stunted tree growing in this place. A strange, terrible burning smell penetrated the carriage despite the thick glass of the windows. I could see vapors rising sluggishly from the earth and writhing along like yellowish snakes. In some places, the ground was as smooth and shiny as glass.

This, then, was the tainted ground, but surely it could not long ago have been true Blacklands.

Now I understood the tension of the horses. It was not the storm they had feared but the poisoned earth they must cross. It was a narrow stretch, and only a short time passed before we returned to a less desolate landscape, but the brief glimpse of the effects of the Great White seared into my mind.

I heard a faint rumbling sound and, looking around again, wondered what could happen next. The noise arose almost from the hills themselves, and a small breeze began to blow. The sky had the dull sheen of polished metal as the wind grew in force. All at once it was cold enough that my breath misted the air inside the carriage.

Then the storm burst over us again. This time there was no rain, just a fierce wind that tossed the cart around like a leaf. The long-suffering trees were bent almost double beneath this fresh onslaught, and I began to understand their ragged appearance. They did well even to survive in this savage land. There seemed something primitive and destructive in the wind, an evil intent I could nearly feel.

Like the rain, it stopped suddenly, and all at once I could hear only the slushy rattle of the wheels as they plowed through the new mud. The sound accomplished what nothing else had been able to do—it woke the guardian.

With a grunt, she sat up and blinked owlishly. "Have we passed the storms?" she asked.

"You mean . . . they're always like that?" I asked.

"If you went back there right now, the storms would still be going on," the guardian confirmed with a shudder of distaste. "They're caused by the Blacklands."

I looked out the window again.

The last stretch of the journey seemed endless, for Obernewtyn was some distance from the tainted pass. The country grew more fertile and ordinary, though very jagged and uneven, with great outcrops of stone rearing up here and there from the dense forest. It was still a hard, wild sort of land, but it seemed fair and rich after the devastated terrain.

My sense of time was utterly confused, but I realized now that night had given way to the early morning, for its dense blackness had transmuted into a frigid, dark blue.

"There," said the guardian suddenly, and I saw a sign swinging between two posts. In dark lettering, it read OBERNEWTYN. KEEP OUT.

The sight of it chilled me more effectively than all

the Blacklands in existence. Just beyond was an iron gate set into a high stone wall. The wall extended as far as I could see in both directions. Enoch pulled the horses up and unlocked the gate. He walked the weary team through, then relocked it from the other side. I wondered why they bothered—surely Obernewtyn's remoteness barred the way more effectively than any locks. I tried to see the house, but thick, ornately clipped trees hid their secret well in the curving drive. Someone had gone to great lengths to keep Obernewtyn from prying eyes.

"Obernewtyn," whispered the guardian, looking out the other window. Her voice was low, as if the somber building that had come into view quelled her as much as it did me. Even the horses seemed to walk softly.

It was a massive construction and outwardly more like a series of bleak buildings pushed haphazardly together than one single mansion. It was constructed of large, rough-hewn blocks of gray stone streaked with flecks of darker stone. Aside from the stone itself, no effort had been made to make one section harmonize with the rest. In some places, it was two or three stories high, and turrets rose up at its corners, with steep little roofs ending in spires. Each wall was pocked with hundreds of slitlike holes that I realized must serve as windows.

The drive curved around an ugly fountain, from which rose a lamppost. Its flame flickered behind gleaming panels, making shadows dance along the walls of the building. Atop a set of wide stone steps, the entrance seemed to move in the shifting light, making me think of an opening maw.

The carriage had drawn to a stop at the foot of the

steps, and Enoch unlocked the door. I climbed out after the guardian. The cold air gusted and made my cloak flap violently enough that I clutched at it, fearing it would be wrenched away from me. The branches of the trees were filled with the blustering wind, and the noise they made seemed a mad whispering that made my skin rise up into gooseflesh.

I shivered and told myself sternly not to let my imagination get the better of me.

Only when we reached the top of the steps did I see that the two broad entrance doors were deeply and intricately carved wood. The beauty of the carvings struck me, particularly because the building itself seemed so utterly utilitarian. I studied them as the guardian rang a bell. Men and all manner of queer beasts were represented, many seeming half man and half beast. Whoever had done the work was a true craftsman, for the expressions on the faces portrayed the essences of the emotions that shaped them. Framing the panels was a wide gilt border decorated with exotic symbols. The symbols seemed to me a sort of scribing, though I could make no sense of them.

At last the doors opened to reveal a tall, thin woman holding a candelabrum. The light shivered and twitched in the wind, giving her gaunt features a curious, almost fluid look. She bent closer, and I wondered if she found me as indistinct in the wavering light. I was too tired to pretend dullness and hoped weariness would do as well.

"You'll get no sense out of her," said Guardian Hester scornfully. "I thought Madam Vega did not intend to bring up any more dreamers. This one doesn't even look strong enough to be a good worker."

The other woman raised her eyebrows disdainfully. "If Madam chose this girl, she will not have done so without purpose," she said very distinctly, and peered into my face in much the same way Madam Vega had at Kinraide, but without any of her hypnotic power.

"Elspeth, this is Guardian Myrna," said Hester.

"You may leave now," the other woman told her abruptly.

"But . . . but I thought, since it was so late . . ." Guardian Hester hesitated and faltered before the gaze of the other.

"It is not permitted for temporary guardians to stay in the main house. You know that. If our arrangement does not please you, I am sure another can be found."

Guardian Hester clasped her hands together. "Please. No. I . . . forgot. I'll go to the farms with the coachman," she said.

Guardian Myrna inclined her head regally after a weighty pause. "You should hurry. So much talk has delayed you, and I think the dogs are out," she said. The other woman paled and hastened to the door. Guardian Myrna watched her go with a cold smile; then she took some keys from her apron pocket. "Come," she said.

We went out a doorway leading off the circular entrance chamber and into a long hall pitted with large doors. Clumsy locks hung from each, and I thought that if this was an indication of the security at Obernewtyn, I would have no trouble getting away. Distantly, I heard the bark of a dog.

The guardian unlocked one of the doors. "Tonight you will sleep here, and tomorrow you will be given a permanent room." She shut the door behind me and bolted it.

I stood a moment in the total darkness, using my mind to ascertain the dimensions of the room. I was relieved to discover that I was alone. It was too cold to get undressed, so I simply slipped my shoes off and climbed into the nearest bed. I drifted uneasily to sleep, thinking I would rather be anywhere than Obernewtyn.

❖ 9 ❖

THE DOOR BANGED violently open.

A girl stood on the stone threshold with a candle in one hand. With her free hand, she continued to hammer loudly at the open door with a peculiar fixed smile on her face.

"What is it?" I said.

She looked at me through lackluster eyes. "I am come . . . I have come . . ." She faltered as though her brain had lost the thread of whatever message she wanted to impart. She frowned. "I have come to . . . to warn you." There was a glimmer in the depth of her muddy eyes, and all at once, I doubted my initial impression that she was defective.

"Warn me about what?" I asked warily.

She made a warding-off movement with her free hand. "Them. You know."

I shook my head. "I don't know. I am new here. Who are you?"

She jerked her head in a spasm of despair, and a look of anguish came over her face. "Nothing! I'm nothing anymore. . . ."

She looked across the room at me and started to laugh. "You should not have come here," she said at last.

"I didn't choose to come here. I am an orphan, and now I am condemned a Misfit."

The girl giggled. "I was no orphan, but I am a Misfit." She laughed again.

Unable to make any sense out of her, I reached out with my thoughts. At once I learned that her name was Selmar and her mind was a charred wreckage. Most of her thought links did not exist, and little remained that was normal. I saw the remnant of someone I could have liked. But whatever she had gone through had left little of that person. Here was a mind teetering on the brink of madness.

Her eyes rolled back in panic, and cursing my stupidity, I realized she could feel me! She must have been one of those people with some fleeting ability. For an instant, her eyes rolled forward, and she looked out with a sort of puzzlement, as if she was struggling to remember something of great importance. But all too quickly, the muddiness in her eyes returned, and with it a pitiful, cowering fear.

"I promise I don't know anything about a map," she whispered.

I stared in bewilderment. What was she talking about now?

"Selmar . . . ," I began, throwing aside my covers and lowering my feet to the cold stone floor.

Before I could say more, a voice interrupted. "Selmar, how is it that you take so long to wake one person?"

It was a sweet, piping voice, high-pitched and querulous. Not a voice to inspire fear, yet, if it were possible, Selmar paled even further as she turned to face the young boy behind her. No more than eleven or twelve years, he was as slender as a wand, with delicate blond curls; slim, girlish shoulders; and large, pale eyes.

"Answer me," he hissed. Selmar swayed as if she would faint, though she was older and bigger than him.

"I . . . I didn't do anything," she gibbered. "She wouldn't wake up."

He clicked his teeth. "You took too long. I see you need a talk with Madam to help you overcome your laziness. I will make sure to arrange it." The sheer maliciousness in his beautiful face angered me.

"It is as she told you," I said, stepping between them. "I had trouble waking, because I arrived so late last night."

Selmar nodded pathetically.

"Well, go on with your duties, then," he conceded with a nasty smile. Selmar turned with a frightened sob and fled down the hall, her stumbling footsteps echoing after her. Chewing his bottom lip, the boy watched her departure with thoughtful eyes.

"What did she say to you?" he asked, turning back to me.

"Nothing," I answered flatly, wondering by what right he interrogated me.

He frowned petulantly. "You're new. You will learn," he said. "Now get up and I will come back for you." He closed the door behind him.

Rummaging angrily through a chest of assorted clothes, I found a cloak. It was freezing within the stone walls, and pale early-morning light spilled in wanly from the room's sole window. There were no shutters, and cold gusts of air swept freely through the opening. I would have liked to look outside, but the window was inaccessible, fashioned long and thin, reaching from above my head almost to the ceiling.

The door opened suddenly. "Come on, then," the blond boy snapped.

As we walked down the hall, I noticed a good deal more than I had the previous night. There were metal candle brackets along the walls, shaped like gargoyles' heads with savage mouths. Cold, greenish drips of wax hung frozen from the gaping jaws. I eyed them with distaste, reflecting that whoever had built Obernewtyn had no desire for homely comfort.

We passed the entrance hall with its heavy front doors and continued along a narrow walkway on the other side.

"Where are you taking me?" I asked.

The boy did not answer, and presently we came to a double set of doors. He opened one with something of a flourish. It opened onto a kitchen, a long, rectangular room with two large dining arbors filled with bench seats and trestle tables. At the far end of the kitchen, almost an entire wall was taken up with a cavernous fireplace. Above it was set an immense mantelshelf, laden with stone and iron pots. From its underside hung a further selection of pans and pannikins. A huge, blackened cauldron was suspended over the flame, and stirring the contents was a woman of mountainous proportions.

Her elbows, though bent, resembled large cured hams, and a large white bow sat on her hips and waggled whenever she moved. The roaring heat of the fire had prevented her from noticing our entrance. Tearing my eyes away, I saw that there were several doors besides the one we had come through and a great number of cupboards and benches. A young girl was sitting at one of these, scraping potatoes, and they sat in two mounds on either side of her. She watched me with currant-like eyes buried in a slab-jowled face. The knife poised above the potato glinted brightly.

"Ma!" she yelled, waving the knife in agitation, throwing its light at me.

The mountain of flesh at the stove trembled, then turned with surprising grace. The woman's face was flushed from the heat and distorted by too many chins, but there was a definite resemblance between her and the girl. The thick ladle in her hand dripped brown gravy, unheeded.

"Ariel!" she cried in dulcet tones. Her accent was similar to Enoch's but less musical. "Dear hinny, I have nowt seen ye in an age. Ye have not deserted me, have ye, sweet boy?"

She gathered him in a bone-crushing embrace and led him to one of the cupboards. She took out a sweet and gave it to him.

"Why, Andra, thank you." Ariel sounded pleased, and I wondered why the cook treated him with such favor. Surely he was only a Misfit, unless he was also an informer. Yet he seemed too arrogant for the latter. Most informers were clinging and contemptible, and even those who used them tended to dislike them.

The girl with the knife giggled violently, and again the blade flashed its silver light. The older woman glared ferociously at her.

"Ye born noddy-headed thing. Shut yer carrying on an' get back to work." The girl's giggles ceased abruptly. Catching sight of me watching her, she scowled as if I were to blame.

72

"Now, Andra," Ariel said. "You recall how I promised you some extra help? Well, I have brought you a new worker."

Responding with enthusiasm, the cook launched herself at him with much lip-smacking. I thought with suppressed glee that it served him right. He caught the amusement on my face. Disentangling himself, he ordered the cook to make sure I worked hard, as I was assuredly lazy and insolent. Andra promised to work my fingers to the bone as he departed with a look of spiteful satisfaction.

As soon as the door closed, her daughter leapt toward me, brandishing her knife. "Misfit pig. What sort of help will she be? Ye can see she don't have a brain in her," she sneered venomously, menacing me with the knife.

The syrupy smile dropped from the cook's face. She crossed the floor in two steps and dealt her daughter a resounding blow with the wooden spoon. "If she has no brains, then she'll be a good match fer ye, fool that ye are, Lila. If Ariel gives us th' gift of a fool, then ye mun show pleasure!" the cook snarled. "Oh, th' trials of my life. Yer no-good father gives me a fool fer a daughter, then disappears. I have to come to th' end of th' Land so ye won't be declared defective. I find a nice powerful boy to bond ye an' yer so stupid I got to do th' charmin' fer ye. Lud knows ye've little enough to offer without gollerin' an' gigglin' like a regular loon," she added succinctly.

With some amusement, I realized that the cook intended a match between her daughter and Ariel. It seemed he wasn't a Misfit. But what sort of power could such a young boy possess?

With a final look of disgust at her daughter, the cook turned to me. "As fer you, no doubt ye are a fool at that. An' work ye hard I will, if that's what Ariel wants. Ye've angered him somehow, an' ye mun pay. He'll see ye do. He ain't one to let petty angers gan away. Ye'll learn," she prophesied.

Turning to the sink, she explained that I was to wash the mountain of dishes and then scour the pots. I looked in dismay at the work ahead. In the orphan homes, there had been a great many of us, and a share in duties was always light. Yet there was nothing to do but obey.

I had been working for hours and had just managed to finish the dishes when the cook announced that the easy work was over since it was nearly time for mid-meal. I felt like weeping. Already I was exhausted, but as Lila and I set the tables, I channeled my despair into fueling a growing hatred of Ariel, whom I regarded as the initiator of my woes. I was hungry, having missed firstmeal, but I dared not complain as I carried bowl after bowl of stew to the tables. Lila moaned endlessly and received endless slaps for her pains. I judged it wiser to hold my tongue.

Presently, the cook rang a bell. Young people of varying ages filed in through the double doors. Soon all the tables were full. The diners did not look at us at all but ate with steady concentration, then left, their seats soon taken by others. The meal consisted of a bowl of thick stew and freshly baked bread. The food smells made me feel dizzy with hunger. In town, food had seldom been this good or this fresh, but we had never had to work too hard. I wondered wistfully what the others did and regretted that I had fallen foul of Ariel.

"Ye gan eat now," the cook said finally, and thrust a generous helping into my hand. My stomach growled in appreciation. I sat at a nearly empty table and devoured the food. Only when I had spooned up the last morsel did I look up.

"Hello," said a soft voice at my elbow. I turned to look at a young blond girl sitting nearby. She smiled, and I was astonished that anyone would ever want to condemn her. Even her ungainly clothes could not hide the delicacy of her features and her slender bones. Her hair was like cream silk. She endured my examination without embarrassment, until it was I who looked away from her clear, naive gaze.

"I am Cameo," she whispered. I looked at her again, and such was the sweetness of her expression that I might have smiled back, but Lila, seated at the end of the table, was watching us.

"I am not interested in your name," I said in a repressive voice, worried that Ariel would punish the girl for her kindness toward me. But when the brightness of her face dimmed, I wished I had not been so terse.

A sharp cuff on the side of my head was the cook's signal that my short respite was over. I rose and began to clear plates. The afternoon was spent washing all the midmeal dishes and scrubbing down the jagged kitchen floor, then serving stew and unwatered milk for nightmeal.

Every bone ached by the time Ariel took me to my permanent room, and I was too exhausted to care that I was not alone. At that moment, the Master of Obernewtyn himself could have been my roommate and met as little response.

· 10 ·

MY INITIAL EXHAUSTION wore off as I became accustomed to the hard physical labor in the kitchen, but it was replaced by a terrible mental despair. I could not endure the thought of going on in such a way forever, and yet there seemed no opportunity of finding Enoch's friend who might be able to help me move to the farms to work.

My sole comfort came from a conversation I had overheard at midmeal one day, which had implied that most of the house workers went down to work on the farms to prepare for the long wintertime. I prayed this was so, and that I would be among those dispatched to the farms. But I had arrived at Obernewtyn in the spring, and my calculations told me no extra workers would be required until the beginning of summerdays.

I shared my sleeping chamber with four other girls, including the strange disturbed girl I had seen on my first morning, Selmar, who now ignored me. Remembering the mess inside her mind, I thought it possible she had simply forgotten our meeting. She was, I noticed, permitted to wander more freely than the rest of us.

There were surprisingly few guardians at Obernewtyn. Most responsibility seemed to be taken by senior and favored Misfits, though none was so favored as Ariel. I had heard nothing of the mysterious master and had seen no sign of Madam Vega.

Altogether, life at Obernewtyn was a matter of grim endurance rather than terror. I thought a good deal about Jes. I had imagined myself a loner, never needing anyone, but now I saw that I had never really experienced loneliness. In Rangorn, there had always been my parents, and in the homes, there had been Jes and later Maruman. I had discounted Jes, but now I often found myself longing to talk to him, even if we spoke of nothing important.

One day late in spring, Ariel came to the kitchen to announce that I was to take a tour of the farms with some other Misfits. Even the knowledge that Ariel would lead the tour could not mar the joy that arose in me at the thought of even a few hours of freedom from the dreary kitchen routine. I had not been outside for so long.

Ariel had instructed me to wait for him in the entrance hall after midmeal. When I arrived, a boy ushered me down several halls and outside into a large enclosed courtyard. Three girls whose faces I recognized from the meal table were waiting already, and soon after a dark-haired boy with a limp arrived. With him was the pretty girl who had spoken to me at my first meal, Cameo. She smiled at me tentatively, but I felt her companion watching me and could not bring myself to respond.

Ariel arrived soon after accompanied by twins—Norselanders, judging by their height and blondness. There were few enough in the highlands for me to be curious about how they had ended up being charged as Misfits. I could not see anything out of the ordinary in their appearance, save that each lacked a hand. I was contemplating entering their minds when the hair on my neck prickled. Turning my head slightly, I saw that the slight, dark-haired boy was still watching me. I scowled at him, suddenly remembering that I had seen him in the dining arbors and he had been watching me then, too. It occurred to me that he might be an informant, and I turned my back on him, resolving to have nothing to do with him.

At last two final Misfits joined us, and Ariel addressed the group. He told us we were being taken on this tour in preparation for working on the farms. I felt a ripple of delight at the news.

Like the kitchen courtyard, the one in which we had gathered was roofed, but now we followed Ariel through a gate into another courtyard that was open to the sky. The sun was shining brightly down on the cobbles, and I turned my face to it and breathed in warm mountain air and tasted the summerdays so soon to come.

Three sides of the courtyard were formed by the high walls of Obernewtyn. Windows pitted the gray expanse like hooded eyes. Above them, the roof sloped steeply so that in wintertime the snow would slide off.

Ariel led us to the fourth wall, beyond which showed the tops of trees. There was no mortar between the bricks of its gateway's arch; rather, it was held up by perfect balance of positioning. Certainly someone had possessed an eye for beauty, I thought, noting its graceful design and remembering the carved doors at the entrance.

I passed through the door beneath the arch expecting to find farms on the other side. Instead, before us rose a thick, impenetrable wall of greenthorn as high as the stone wall behind us. Peer as I might, I could not tell what lay beyond it, but a small grassy path ran to the left and the right. Ariel steered us to the left, and we followed the path a short way until it turned sharply to the right. We walked a few steps and came to a fork. Each way looked exactly alike, bordered on either side by the towering greenthorn hedge.

By now, the powerful exotic odor of the greenthorn and the sameness of the surroundings had completely confused my sense of direction, and I realized the shrubbery was actually a maze. I could not even use my powers to feel out the way ahead, because they were befuddled by the heavy scent in the air. Crushed, the thorn provided a painkiller, but in such concentration, the scent alone seemed to have a slight numbing effect on my mind. The maze was large and labyrinthine, and if Ariel had left us alone, I doubt whether we would have found our way out at all.

It was with some relief that we came around a corner to see the stone wall with its arched gateway. It was not until we had gone through it that I realized it was a different door than the one we'd entered. We had come right through the maze to the other side, and before us lay the vast farmlands of Obernewtyn.

I gazed around in amazement. Neat fields extended for leagues in all three directions, and there were barns and fences and livestock everywhere. Dozens of Misfits were working, repairing fences or building them, herding and raking. To the far left was an orchard, and there was the unmistakable scent of apples and plums.

Ariel led us along one of the many dirt paths from the maze toward a group of buildings. I hung back until the dark-haired boy went ahead of me, noting that he had a pronounced limp, though he seemed to have no trouble keeping pace.

"The maze door is always locked," Ariel said over his shoulder as we walked. "And there are few at Obernewtyn who know the way through. To stray from the path means death." The thought that anyone would choose to enter the fragrant green maze without a guide made me shudder. Ariel went on to explain that the buildings we approached were where the animals were kept during the wintertime, and those beyond were enormous storage silos.

"As far as you can see in all directions and much farther belongs to Obernewtyn and, as such, is contained within our walls," Ariel said. "We are almost completely self-sufficient here, as we must be, for in wintertime we are completely blocked off from the lowlands by snow. During that season, everyone will work in the house, spinning and weaving and preparing goods for trading when the spring comes. This enables us to purchase what we cannot produce. Before the wintertime, all the food in those silos must be transported to the main house."

We passed a massive shed that smelled strongly of animals. Ariel wrinkled his nose, but I breathed in deeply, because it reminded me of Rangorn.

"Those are the livestock storage houses. The grain and grasses in those must be enough to feed all the animals throughout the wintertime. Some of the cows and poultry are transferred to the house courtyards to provide meat and eggs and milk until spring."

There was no doubt that it was a highly efficient concern, and the surplus sold must more than cover the few things Obernewtyn wanted. I wondered what happened to the rest of the profits. No doubt some of it was used in purchasing more Misfits.

Far to the west, beyond the distant line of the wall around Obernewtyn, was a savage line of mountains. There were more mountains to the east. Busy with my own thoughts, I did not notice Ariel had been observing me.

"I see you are interested in the mountains beyond our borders," he sneered. "Look all you please, for you will never see them at less of a distance. Those mountains mean freedom and death for those who attempt to reach them."

A raucous squealing from behind us broke the tension. We followed Ariel toward a small shed, but before we reached it, a man came out carrying a small pig. As he approached, I could see that he was not a full-grown man at all but a well-built youth of about nineteen. He set the pig down in a small pen and wiped his hands on his trousers before turning to us. His greeting to Ariel was amicable but reserved; he seemed wary of the younger boy. I decided to probe him to find out why, when a strange thing happened.

He was telling Ariel about the pig he had just delivered when he broke off midsentence to stare at me with jade green eyes. Some instinct of danger made me fear I had betrayed myself, though I had only skirted the conscious thoughts that echoed his speech, and I had found no sign he was mind-sensitive. I expected him to denounce me, but instead he seemed suddenly aware that he in turn was watched. He then let his eyes rove over our entire group, but I felt sure he did this only to cover the attention he had paid me.

Ariel's eyes passed from me to the youth thoughtfully. "This is Rushton," he said to the group. "He is our farm overseer."

Startled, I realized this was Enoch's friend. The dark youth did not have the air of a Misfit, but Ariel did not choose to tell us his exact status. The overseer gave us a description of the farms and crops and the animals thereon, before leaving us to Ariel. His eyes flickered at me once more as he departed, but I was careful to keep my expression bland.

That night, my dreams were full of shadowed green eyes conveying messages I could not understand. When I woke the following morning, Selmar and one of the other girls eyed me oddly, and I knew I must have talked in my sleep, though I could hardly have said much to incriminate myself.

I told myself it did not matter if the overseer had dimly sensed my intrusion, for he would surely have forgotten me by the time I was sent to the farms to work. But that morning, Ariel was waiting for me in the kitchen and bade me sit down to firstmeal rather than serve it.

I was to begin work on the farms that very day.

· 11 ·

THAT FIRST DAY working on the farms, I had my first glimpse of a Guanette bird. It was a surprising start to a surprising day.

I had been standing alone in the courtyard outside the maze when the bird flew straight up from behind the wall into the silver-streaked, dawn-gray sky. Uttering a long, lonely call, it flew in a graceful arc toward the northwest. I recognized the bird, though I had never seen a picture of one, by its massive wingspan and the brilliant red of its underbelly. As it crossed the line where the far mountains touched the sky, the sun rose in fiery splendor as if to welcome it. The enormous bird flew across the face of the sun, shimmered, and seemed to dissolve.

"Fair mazer it is," said a voice behind me. I turned to see the thin, dark-haired boy who had stared at me so unnervingly the previous day. But now all of his attention was fixed on the Guanette bird. I was startled to see the frank delight in his expression and wondered if he was an informer after all. Behind him was a slightly older boy with a tall, angular body, a rather big nose, and countless freckles struggling to cover his face. He was looking at me with such a peculiar intensity that I stiffened and glared at him indignantly.

Catching my expression, the thin boy turned to his companion and poked him in the chest. "Can't ye feel how uncomfortable she is, ye great gawk?" he asked him. He turned to me and said cheerfully, "Dinna worry about Dameon. He's as blind as a bat."

Horribly embarrassed, I was shamed to think of the icy look I had given him and was thankful he could not see me.

Dameon grinned apologetically. "I'm sorry if I seemed to stare," he said disarmingly, and held his hand out. Startled, I took his hand and wondered at his elegant manner and grace of speech.

"An' I'm Matthew," said the dark-haired boy. "An' you're Elspeth."

I did not know what to say, for his knowledge of my name suggested he had made inquiries about me, yet he did not act like an informant.

"What were you both admiring?" Dameon asked, before I could decide how to respond.

Matthew answered. "We saw a Guanette bird, an' ye know how rare those are. It came from near th' maze. Queer to see one here, though. They dinna usually come down from the high mountains."

The door to the inner courtyard opened, and a group of other Misfits arrived, most of them those who had come on the tour the day before. Ariel arrived last with Cameo in tow. He unlocked the maze door, then relocked it when we had gone through. As he took the lead, I moved to follow, but Matthew caught my arm and held me back until the others had passed. The twins went last, looking at us curiously. Furious, I shook Matthew's hand off and followed them, wishing that I had completely ignored him as my instincts had warned. Did he not understand the danger in doing anything that drew attention?

We walked in silence for a bit; then Cameo began to chatter to Ariel. With her masking prattle, the twins began to talk in low, intense voices. Curiosity made me send out a probe. They were planning some sort of escape, so I withdrew smartly. I didn't even want to think of escapes, intended or otherwise.

Matthew came to walk beside me, and I glared at him, determined to snub any further attempt at friendship—if that was what he wanted.

"Can you hear me?" asked a voice in my thoughts.

Shocked, I stumbled. Righting myself, I fought to calm my clamoring thoughts. I told myself sternly that I had imagined Matthew's voice inside my mind, but now he reached out and put his hand on my arm. "I thought so," he said quietly. "I sensed you 'listening' to the twins. But I suspected ye before that." He was positively delighted.

I could only feel numb. Even surrounded by Misfits, I had never really thought there would be anybody else like me. "I . . . I don't understand," I said doggedly.

Matthew smiled again in an impish, knowing way. "I thought there was only me and me mam who could do it. Then for the last few sevendays, I began to feel like I did when me mam was about, and I started wonderin' if there was another. I felt it during meals, an' I was gannin' through everyone, dippin' into their minds to see if they could hear me. I couldn't reach ye, though, for ye've a powerful shield. I realized the only way I would ken for sure was to catch ye in the act of farseeking. So I waited, and now I know, Elf."

I shivered at the added proof of his intrusion into

my mind, for how else could he have known Jes's nick-name for me?

"It is dangerous to talk of such things here," I whispered, for I realized there was no point in pretending. It was too late to be cautious. But could he be trusted? I reached into his mind some little way, intending only to find out if there was any chance of betrayal. But before I could learn what I wanted to know, Matthew's eyes narrowed, and I sensed a slight withdrawal in him.

"Interestin'," he whispered. "Ye've just tried to deep-probe me like my mam used to do. I can't do that, and I couldn't stop ye if ye were determined. Ye mun be very strong." He looked suddenly pensive. "Now that I think of it, I can almost understand why those idiots from the village were afraid of me. 'Tis a queer thing to ken yer thoughts are on show. Dameon here has some power, too, but it is not farseeking or deep probing. It's something to do with being able to feel what people are feeling." Matthew shrugged as if he did not think it a very useful ability.

My mind reeled with the things he said. In a few moments, he had changed my life. I had so long believed I was a lone freak with the ability to read the thoughts of other people and of beasts. A strange, almost frightening thought came to me then: if there were three of us, there might be more. There must be more. Belatedly, it occurred to me that I had been rude to dip into Matthew's mind. This sudden desire not to invade the thoughts of another person was new and told me that I had accepted something I had previously thought impossible. I was no longer alone.

"We'll manage canny between us," Matthew was saying, still in that barely audible voice. "I'd be pleased, though, if ye'd teach me how to shield so well, fer I can't believe that shield of yours is any accident," he added humbly. I looked into his bright, intelligent face, and it was as if some wall in me crumbled.

"I will teach you," was all I said, but with those words it was as if I peeled off a layer of skin. Matthew beamed, seeming to understand the momentousness of sharing for the first time, and I thought of Jes and wished he could know what I had discovered.

"And Dameon?" Matthew asked anxiously, breaking into mindspeak.

I turned slightly to watch Dameon's graceful progress behind us and sent out a gentle probe. He flinched and stumbled, and I withdrew hurriedly.

"I'm sorry," I whispered, but he shook his head.

"I was just surprised. It's stronger than when Matthew does it," he said, and smiled. "I can feel your curiosity," he laughed. "It's almost as bad as his. I call my own ability empathy."

"He does that all th' time," Matthew reassured me aloud. "He picks up th' weirdest things. No words, though, an' he's deaf as a doorpost to other things."

"Quiet back there!" Ariel shouted, effectively silencing the entire group. I hoped Matthew would be careful, and to my relief, he said nothing more and dropped back to walk with Dameon. He sent a silent promise that we would meet again soon, when it was safe.

Busy with my thoughts, I cannoned into one of the twins, who had stopped in front of me. We had reached the end of the maze.

Ariel led us out and told us to wait by the maze gate until Rushton came to collect us. Matthew and Dameon made no move to join me, so I took their cue and stayed where I was. The sun had risen quite high now, and though the grass was still dew-soaked and the shadows long, the air smelled delicious with the mingled farm smells.

I glanced back at Matthew and, seeing his sober expression, I had an unaccountable desire to make a face at him. I was amazed at the warmth of my feelings, but as the farm overseer approached from the direction of the sheds, I felt a moment of apprehension. Though this time he paid no particular attention to me, there was an aura of power about him, and I was reminded of something Maruman had once said about wild animals— that even the most gentle was not quite safe. That was how Rushton struck me—as if one might run a great risk in simply knowing him. Yet when he began assigning tasks, his apparent boredom reassured me.

Dameon, Matthew, and others were sent over to a large building that he called the drying shed. Cameo and the twins were sent across to the orchards. Then only two of us remained. The other girl was to feed the pigs, Rushton said, and I was to clean out the stables. He gave me an expressionless look with his bold green eyes and told me to wait inside until he returned.

A large dog lay against a wall just inside the stables. He opened his eyes as I entered and watched me sit on a bale of hay.

"Greetings," I thought on impulse.

His eyes widened, and he looked around before deciding I was the only one there. "Did you speak, funaga?" he asked with mild surprise.

I nodded. "I am Elspeth," I sent. "May I know your name?"

"I am called Sharna," he sent. "What manner of funaga are you?"

"I am a funaga like other funagas," I replied formally.

"I have heard your name before," he sent unexpectedly. "A cat spoke it."

"Maruman!" I projected a picture with the name, but Sharna was unresponsive.

"I did not see this mad cat who seeks a funaga. I heard it from a beast who heard it from another."

"Do you know where the cat was seen?" I asked excitedly.

"Who knows where a cat goes?" he sent philosophically. "The story was only told to me as a curiosity. Whoever heard of a cat looking for a funaga? I thought it a riddle."

Rushton entered the stable then. He looked about sharply as if sensing something had been going on, then he tersely told me to follow him.

If he had shown an interest in me the day before, today he seemed at pains to assure me of his total lack of interest. "The stables have to be cleaned every second day," he said in a bored voice as we entered one of the pens. A rich loamy smell rushed out to greet me. I watched as the overseer demonstrated how to catch hold of the horse's halter and lead it out. The horses were to be released into the yard leading off the stables, he explained, their halters removed and hung on a hook. Once a horse had been led out, Rushton gave me a broom, a rake, and a pan, taking up a long-handled fork himself.

"You have to lift the manure out in clumps and drop

it in the pan, along with the dirtiest hay." Deftly he slid the prongs of the fork under some manure and threw it neatly into the pan. "When you've done all that, rake the rest of the hay to one side, then fork in some fresh stuff." He forked hay from a nearby pile onto the floor with economical movements. It looked easy.

"You lay the old hay over the new; if you don't, the horse will eat it." He handed the fork to me. "There are twelve stables in this lot, so you'd better get on with it. Come and get me at the drying shed if you have any trouble getting the horses out." I nodded, and briefly those inscrutable eyes searched mine, then he turned on his heel and left.

I turned and surveyed the stables.

"You would do well to mindspeak to them first," Sharna commented from his corner. Taking his advice, I approached the nearest box and greeted its occupant, a dappled mare with a large, comfortable rear. She flicked her tail and turned to face me.

"Who are you?" she asked with evident amusement. "I have spoken to many odd creatures in my time but never a funaga. I suppose you are behind this." She directed the latter thought to Sharna, who had ambled over to stand beside me. The mare leaned her long nose close to my face and snorted rudely. "I suppose you want to put me out? Well, I'm not having that thing on my head. Just open the door and I'll walk out."

I did as she asked, hoping Rushton would not come back and catch me disobeying his instructions. Sharna muttered about the mare's bossiness, but I ignored him and concentrated on copying Rushton's movements as I mucked out the box.

Except for a big, nasty black horse whom Sharna

said had been badly mistreated by a previous master, the rest of the horses proved cooperative on the condition I did not use their halters. I had finished and was leaning on a post watching the horses graze when Rushton returned.

"You have been uncommonly swift," he said suspiciously. The smile fell from my face as I realized I had been stupid.

"Too quick to believe, even if Enoch did recommend you," he added.

And as I looked into his hard face, I was afraid.

PART II

◆

HEART OF THE DARKNESS

◆ 12 ◆

"WELL?" RUSHTON INQUIRED grimly.

"I . . . my father kept horses," I lied, hoping he did not know how young I had been orphaned.

"And you did not think to mention it during my instruction?" he asked. There was a speculative gleam in his eyes as I shrugged awkwardly. "All right. There are packages of food for midmeal out by the maze gate. Go and eat, and I'll find something else for you to do in the afternoon," he said.

I left as fast as I could to escape those curious, watchful eyes.

The packages lay on a piece of cloth on the ground next to a large bucket of milk covered with a piece of gauze. I scooped up a mug of milk but avoided the squashy packages I recognized from my days in the kitchen as bread and dripping. Propping myself against a rain barrel in the sun, I again berated myself for my foolishness in working so quickly. I could have been with Sharna and the horses all day, but instead Rushton was sure to give me some horrible job now that he thought I had wasted his time.

I turned my thoughts to Maruman and wondered if he had been in the mountains. I doubted it. He could not have crossed the tainted ground on foot, and I did not think Enoch's carriage had returned since my arrival, because I had noticed no new faces at meals.

I was so deep in thought that I did not see Matthew and Dameon approach, and I jumped as their shadows fell across my lap. They sat beside me, and I felt as though everything had changed in a matter of hours. Only yesterday this casual intrusion would have annoyed me, but I found I did not resent the company of this odd pair.

Nevertheless, I felt bound to point out to them that we made ourselves vulnerable by showing friendship openly. "I'm not saying I don't want your company, but maybe it's not a good idea to be so obvious," I ventured, looking around doubtfully at Misfits sitting nearby.

Matthew shrugged. "Elspeth, yer thinkin' like an orphan. We are Misfits now. What more could they do?"

Burn us, I thought, but did not say it, for that seemed unlikely now. And he was right. I *had* been thinking like an orphan. The two boys unwrapped their lunches. Dameon rewrapped his with a grimace, but Matthew ate his with a bored expression.

"Have ye come across old Larkin yet?" Matthew asked presently. I shrugged, saying I hadn't seen anyone but Rushton. "Nivver mind," Matthew laughed. "Yer bound to see him soon. Ye'll know when ye do. He's not th' sort ye could easily forget."

"Who is he, a guardian?" I asked curiously.

"There are only three permanent guardians up here," Dameon explained. "The others come and go. They don't last long, though." I thought of Guardian Myrna's treatment of the hapless Hester and did not wonder.

"Strictly speakin', Larkin is a Misfit, but he's much

older than the rest of us," Matthew said. "Do you notice how there are no older Misfits? They send them to th' Councilfarms. But Larkin has been here forever, and probably the Councilfarms dinna want someone as old as him. But he's a queer fey old codger. An' rude as they come—I'm not even sure I like him exactly. But if ye can get him talkin', he has some interesting ideas."

"I don't suppose half of it is true," Dameon said with a grin.

But Matthew refused to be drawn. "I daresay he does make a lot of it up. But he knows a lot, too. An' some of th' things he says about th' Beforetime make a lot more sense than the rubbish the Herders put about. There's no harm in hearin' ideas . . . unless ye happen to be blind in more ways than one," he added with an oblique glance at Dameon. I thought it a rather tactless jibe, but Dameon only laughed.

"So where is he, then?" I asked crossly, somehow envious of their casual friendship.

"Well, he's nowt a man to blow th' whistle an' bang th' drum. In fact, I sometimes think he'd like to be invisible. But he works on th' farms, so ye'll meet him soon enough, doubtless," Matthew said.

I thought of something else. "Tell me, the overseer—is he a Misfit?"

"Nobody really seems to know," Matthew said. "I asked Larkin once, an' he told me to mind my business."

Dameon nodded. "He might work for pay, like the temporary guardians. But I don't know. Whenever I'm near him, I sense a ferocious purpose and drive, though to what I do not know."

"What about Ariel, then?" I asked.

97

"I hate him," Matthew said with cold venom. I was taken aback at his vehemence, and Dameon actually flinched.

"I'm sorry," Matthew said contritely. He looked at me. "Ye have to be careful about what ye feel. Sometimes things hurt him."

"Burns," mumbled Dameon. "Hate always burns."

I thought that was true enough.

"Ariel is a Misfit, but he has great authority here," Dameon explained. "He is Madam Vega's personal assistant. I have heard that he started off as an informer and proved especially good at it."

"Do you . . . I mean, what do you feel when you're near him?" I asked.

"Lots of things, and none of them good. The ugliness is deep down in him. It's like being near something that smells sweet, and then you realize it's that sweet smell that rotten things sometimes get," he said, then he sighed as if annoyed by his vague explanation. But I found it a curiously apt description.

"And you say Larkin has been here for a long time?" I said, changing the subject because Dameon was looking pale. His powers seemed to demand more of him than mine did of me.

"Since this place was built," Matthew said extravagantly. "An' if ye want to know about people . . ."

I shook my head hastily. "Oh, it wasn't so much people as Obernewtyn itself I was thinking about. It seems such an odd place. Why would anyone build here in the first place? And when did it become a home for Misfits, and why? There is some kind of secret here, I sense it. I don't know why I should care. The world is full of secrets, but this nags at me."

"I feel that, too," Matthew said eagerly. "As if something is going on underneath all these everyday things."

"It makes me cold to listen to you two," Dameon said suddenly. "I don't deny that I have felt something, too. Not the way you two do, and not by using any power. But a blind person develops an instinct for such things, and mine tells me there is some mystery here. Something big. But some things are better left unknown." His words were grim, and I found myself looking round nervously.

Dameon went on. "Sometimes I am afraid for people like you who have to know things. And there's no point in my even warning you that finding out can sometimes be a dangerous thing. Your kind will dig and hunt and worry at it until one day you will find what is hidden, waiting for you."

I shivered violently.

"Curiosity killed th' cat," Matthew said. I looked up, startled, thinking of Maruman. "That's what Larkin told me once. He said it was an Oldtime saying."

"And how would he know Oldtime sayings?" I asked, throwing off the chill cast over me by Dameon's words.

"From books," Matthew said calmly. "He keeps them hidden, but I've seen them."

"It seems like a silly sort of saying to me," I said, though I was fascinated at the thought of hidden books.

"Well, sayin' it cleared the ice out of me blood." Matthew looked at Dameon, who seemed preoccupied with his own thoughts since he had uttered his chilling little speech. "Ye fair give me th' creeps talkin' that way," he added.

"Do you know, I was just thinking," Dameon said. Matthew gave me a "not again" look. "I once thought it was the end of the world to be sent here, the end of everything. But here I sit, content, and with two friends, and I wonder."

"I know what ye mean," Matthew agreed. "I near died of fright when Madam Vega picked me to come here. But now I sometimes get th' funny feeling that this, all along, was where I was meant to come."

I said nothing but thought of Maruman saying that my destiny waited for me in the mountains.

"Yet, it is not freedom," Dameon added softly, and we both looked at him. The bell to end midmeal rang, seeming to underline his words.

"Ah well. Back to work," Matthew said glumly, and pulled Dameon to his feet. With a wave, they went back across the fields.

Rushton came to stand beside me as I watched them go. "I see you accomplish many things quickly," he sneered. "I should have thought the orphan life would have taught you caution in choosing companions."

I said nothing.

"Well, this afternoon, you can show your talents at milking. I don't suppose your father had cows as well as horses?" he added.

I shook my head and fell into step behind him, hoping he was not to be my teacher for the afternoon. I was beginning to ache from the morning's work. We went to a big barn, which Rushton said was the dairy. A bearded man was sitting on a barrel near the entrance.

"Louis, this is Elspeth Gordie," Rushton told the man. "You can have her for the afternoon."

The old man's deeply weathered face twitched, but

it was too wrinkled to tell if he smiled or not. "I hope she's quicker than th' last," the old man said abruptly.

"Oh, she's quick all right," Rushton said pointedly as the old man got to his feet and led me inside. I looked back, expecting to see the overseer's departing back, but he stood there watching me.

Louis instructed me on milking cows, thoroughly and at such length that I began to wonder if he thought me a half-wit. I understood what he meant long before he completed his explanations.

He reminded me of a tortoise. That is not to suggest, however, that there was anything foolish or absurd about him. Tortoises, though slow, are dignified and self-sufficient. On the other hand, I had the distinct but unfounded impression that his thoughts were not nearly as slow as his appearance would have me believe. He grunted his satisfaction when I demonstrated that I could milk the cow according to his instructions. Then he gave me terse directions on emptying the bucket into the correct section of a separation vat.

"Nowt like it," he said wistfully, and I jumped because so far, the only words he had spoken had been orders. He pointed to the milk, and I nodded, wondering if he was slightly unbalanced. "Ye don't gan milk like that in th' towns. Watery pale stuff tasting of drainpipes," he said, patting the cow's rump complacently. "Ye mun call me Larkin," he said.

"Oh," I said, startled at the realization that this was the man who Matthew and Dameon had told me about.

"Lead her out, then," Louis said easily.

Leading the cow outside to graze, I returned to find that Louis had brought in a second cow and was emptying the bucket of milk into a wooden vat.

"Dinna mix th' vats up," Louis cautioned me, and bid me get on with milking.

Sitting at the milking stool, I grasped the cow's udders. I apologized to her as I began to milk her, but she merely sighed and told me that it was a relief. Louis came to watch me, and I wondered if permission to use his last name was a good or bad sign. It was hard to be sure how he felt with that beard and his leathery face. As I milked, I took the opportunity to question the cow about him. Like most cows, she was a slow, amiable creature without much brain. But she was fond of Louis, and that disposed me to like him.

"Niver gan done that way!" Louis snapped, and I jumped. I had fallen into a pleasant drowse, leaning my head on the cow's warm, velvety flank. As I sat up and went on milking, Louis pulled a box up and sat, scraping at a pipe.

"I suppose you've been here a long time," I ventured. He nodded, still busy with his pipe. "I suppose you would know just about everybody here...." I looked up quickly, and he seemed unperturbed by my questions. But I decided it might be better to ask him about himself before questioning him about anything else. "Were you born in the highlands?" I asked daringly.

Louis chewed the end of his pipe and looked at me thoughtfully. "I were born here," he said. I stared but he did not elaborate. "After this place became what it is now, I went to work in the highlands, but I dinna fit there, an' soon enow they put me right back here." He gave a smile that was both sly and childishly transparent. "Them smart townsfolk think they know everything. They think they can keep things th' same forever.

But change comes an' things have gone too far to drag 'em back to what they was. Every year there be more Misfits an' seditioners, an' one day that Council will find there's more in th' prisons than out." He chuckled.

Matthew had been right about the old man's interesting ideas. I wondered how I could get him to talk about Obernewtyn. "This place . . . it's been here a long time," I said.

He shrugged, hardly seeming to hear the question. I decided to try another tack. "Do you know Ariel? And Selmar?" I asked.

He nodded, but his eyes had grown wary, and I wondered which name had produced the change. "Oh, aye. I know them all, an' more. Selmar's a poor sad thing now. Ye'd nowt know her if ye could see how she were when she first came. An' she were th' hope of Obernewtyn . . . ," he said bitterly.

I frowned in puzzlement, for the girl that had hammered at my door that first day seemed utterly defective. Apparently she had not been born that way. I was about to ask Louis what had happened to her when he suddenly stood up, knocked his pipe out, and ordered me tersely to get on with the milking and take myself back to the maze gate when I was finished. He stamped on the glowing ashes and walked away.

When I had finished the milking and washed the buckets, I came out of the barn forlornly, thinking I had a bad habit of annoying the wrong people. I had sat down outside the barn to rest for a moment when I heard a soft footfall.

"Don't tell me you are tired!" came Rushton's mocking voice. I looked up to find the overseer looking down at me, and suddenly anger surged through me.

"People like you are the worst sort," I said in a low voice that seemed to surprise him with its intensity. "You make everything so much worse with your sneering and snide comments. I do my work. Why don't you just leave me alone?"

For a moment, he actually seemed taken aback; then he shrugged. "I hardly think the opinions of one Misfit will trouble me too much," he said. "Now get up. It is time for you to return to the house."

I got to my feet, knowing I had been stupid to speak up as I had, for an overseer would certainly have power enough to make me regret my outburst. The weariness in my body had somehow crept into my spirit, and I said nothing as we made our way to the maze gate, collecting others along the way. Rushton left us with an older girl who unlocked the gate and led us through the maze.

I did not see Matthew or Dameon, and guessed they had gone back with an earlier group. I felt isolated and dispirited. I thought of Enoch's warm recommendation of Rushton, wondering how they had become friends. Certainly it was impossible to imagine the cold, stern Rushton as anyone's friend.

Thinking of Enoch made me think of Maruman and wonder again where the story of a cat searching for a funaga had originated. If only he were safe with the friendly old coachman. Surely it must be so. The coach horses could easily have told one of the animals on the farm about Maruman when Enoch came to Obernewtyn. But again I remembered that I'd seen no new faces recently. And what other reason would Enoch have for coming to Obernewtyn save to deliver a new Misfit?

◆ 13 ◆

I WAS IN one of the tower rooms at Obernewtyn, a room I had not seen before. It was very small and round. There was a tiny window and a door leading to a balcony.

I was about to go outside when I heard voices and realized I had no right to be there. I cringed against a wall, seeking a place to hide. Then I heard a strange keening noise, a grinding sound like metal against metal, only more musical. There was a note in the noise not unlike a scream.

As I drifted out of the dream, the noise seemed to carry on into my waking state. It was a tantalizingly familiar sound, I realized, not something that I had ever heard in my life, but a sound that oft came to me in dreams.

Thunder rolled in the air.

I opened my eyes to see Cameo hasten into my room. I usually woke to the sound of the bedroom door being unlocked in the morning, but I knew I had overslept when I saw the other beds were empty.

"Are you all right?" Cameo said. "You yelled out, and I was passing. . . ." She faltered, unsure of her welcome.

I forced a smile. "I was having a nightmare that a

horse was about to trample me," I said lightly as I climbed out of bed.

Uninvited, Cameo sat and watched me dress. She was very pale. "I have dreams that frighten me, too," she said in a grave tone. I stared at her curiously, but she seemed lost in her thoughts.

"Nightmares," I suggested gently.

A tear slid down her nose and dripped onto her clasped hands. "True dreams," she said. "That's why they sent me here. But they are getting worse. I dream something is trying to get me, something horrible and evil." She dropped her head into her hands and wept in earnest.

I patted her shoulder awkwardly. "Perhaps it only feels like a true dream. I have heard it's hard to tell," I said.

She looked up, and a wave of exhaustion crossed her face, making her look suddenly much older. "I am so tired," she said. "I try not to go to sleep, because I'm scared of what I will dream."

I did not know what to say. She reminded me of Maruman in one of his fits, and there was never anything I could do to soothe him when he was under the sway of his strange dreams. Then the hair on my neck prickled, and I looked up to see Ariel watching us from the open doorway.

"What is going on here?" he demanded.

I glanced at Cameo, who sat white and silent, staring at her feet, and I remembered how she had happily chattered to Ariel when he had taken us to the farms. Yet now she would not look at him, and he regarded her like a hunter deciding when to loose the killing arrow. Perhaps he had appeared in her true dreams.

"What did you want?" I asked insolently, wanting to draw his attention from Cameo. He gave me a hard look, then told us to hurry up and assemble at the inner maze gate, for we had already missed firstmeal.

Thunder rumbled all morning over the farms but no rain fell. The sky was a thick, congested gray with streaks of milky white clouds strung low in fibers from east to west. I ate midmeal with little appetite, despite having missed firstmeal. A foreboding feeling filled me. I could not talk to Dameon and Matthew about Cameo, because two other boys sat near us and engaged them in conversation.

Before we went back to work, Matthew did manage to tell me quickly that the boys he had been talking to were acquaintances of Rushton's. Matthew found their sudden friendliness suspicious.

"We'd better be careful," he warned. "I wouldn't like anyone to find out what we can do. I can just imagine the doctor wanting to experiment on us."

His words made my blood run cold. "Doctor?" I asked, the word unfamiliar.

"It is an Oldtime word meaning a person who studies healing," Matthew said.

I wanted to ask more, but there was no chance, for Rushton had arrived and was looking pointedly at us.

Since my outburst at the milking sheds several weeks before, the overseer had been curt, but he did not say anything to me apart from giving me instructions. I had expected some punishment, but nothing happened. That afternoon I was to spend with Louis Larkin learning how to make butter. I spent quite a lot of time with Louis and was looking after the horses and some goats. Best of all, I liked the time I spent alone with the horses. Sharna, who lived with Louis, usually spent that time with me.

I spent midmeals with Dameon and Matthew, and when it was safe, we talked, insatiably curious about the very different lives each of us had lived. Matthew had come from the highlands not too far from Guanette and had been able to hide his abilities under his mother's guidance. After she died, he had lived alone in her shack, poaching and fishing and generally living close to the bone, and he developed a reputation for being odd. A group of village boys constantly tormented him. Finally, several of the ringleaders in the gang came to harm. One fell from a roof, and another ate poisoned fish. The village called in the Council and claimed Matthew was dangerous. No one could explain how Matthew, with his lame foot, had hurt the boys, but the Council had been convinced, and he was declared a Misfit.

Astonishingly, Dameon was the son of a Councilman, who had left him vast properties upon his death. But a cousin had conspired to have him declared a Misfit. I was amazed at Dameon's lack of resentment. But he said he had never really felt like a Councilman's son. Because of his ability, he had always felt less than certain about his future. "And, after all, despite my cousin's lies, I *am* a Misfit," he had laughed.

Whenever Cameo came to work on the farms, she would join us. I had thought I would have to argue for her inclusion, since she had no abilities beyond dreaming true, but as it turned out, Matthew was quite fond of her, and Cameo swiftly came to adore him. I wondered what Dameon felt of what was growing between them, thinking it must be odd always to be feeling what other people felt. I was curious how he could tell the difference between other people's feelings and his own.

Midway through one afternoon later that week, Matthew came to the milking shed with a message for Louis and stayed on talking. Usually Louis discouraged gossip during work time, but that day he seemed inclined to conversation.

"Any news?" Matthew asked casually.

Louis was at times a fountain of highland news. It was hard to tell where he got it from, since he appeared to hate almost everyone. I suspected some of it came via Enoch, who was certain to know the old Misfit.

"Nowt much," the old man answered Matthew.

Matthew grinned at me and waited, and presently the old man went on. "Mind ye, rumor has it something is gannin on in th' highlands." Our interest quickened as he took his pipe out, for it was a sure sign he was in an expansive mood.

"I've known for an age something was up," he continued. "Too many strangers up in the high country, sayin' they lived out a way when it was a lie. 'Tis nowt enough just to listen to what people tells ye. Ye have to look in their eyes an' watch what they do. An' them folk belongs to th' towns."

I exchanged a puzzled look with Matthew as Louis relit his pipe.

"But why would they lie?" Matthew prompted.

"Think, boy," Louis retorted with sudden scorn. "What would towns folk be doin' up here to begin' with? They're up to some mischief."

"I heard Henry Druid lived up there still, that he wasn't dead. Maybe the Council is sending people to look for him," I suggested.

The old man looked at me sharply. " 'Tis nowt th' Council; I'll say that straight. They stay away from th' mountains. They get paid to stay out."

"I nivver heard the Druid was alive," Matthew said, looking at me curiously.

"A man like Henry Druid would not be easy to kill," Louis said, almost as if he knew the man.

Matthew looked at me, sending a quick thought that trouble in the highlands would detract attention from any escapes. We had spoken of escape, but not with any real intention. Yet there was a seriousness in his mind that told me he had thought of it more often than I'd realized.

Matthew persisted. "Th' last trouble in the high country was his defection, wasn't it?"

Louis frowned. "Aye. That'd be some ten years ago now. A long time ago past," he said after a pause.

"Maybe he's planning to attack the Council," Matthew said. "For revenge."

Louis shook his head. "Henry Druid must be over forty now. Not a hothead anymore. He was smart, I heard, and smart turns into cunning when ye get old. He'd never win in an outright battle against th' soldier-guards. He'd find some other way. Though he would hate th' Council enough, to be sure. His son an' one of his daughters were killed in th' troubles," Louis added.

"What was it all over anyway?" asked Matthew.

"Nobody knows for sure what started it," Louis answered. "Ye'll hear th' Council say he was a seditious rebel settin' to take over an' drag the Land back into the

Age of Chaos, but that's only one side to th' story, an' Henry Druid ain't here to talk in his defense. But he was a scholar, not a soldier. I dinna think he would even consider war. Not unless he were sure of winnin'."

"I heard he was a Herder," I said. "No wonder there was such a fuss. It was all over forbidden books, wasn't it?"

Louis nodded his head approvingly. "Aye. That's what began it. The Council decided to burn all Oldtime books. Henry Druid had a huge collection of 'em, an' he looked after th' Herder library, too. The Herders agreed with the Council, but Henry Druid refused. He was a popular man, an' he called on friends to help him. I dinna think he had any idea of what would happen. The soldierguards killed some of his friends and burned his whole house down, books an' all. The Herder Faction disowned him, and they were plannin' to execute him as an example. But he escaped with some followers, an' no one's seen them since. Least-ways, no one who's talkin'," he added craftily. "It seemed a good idea at th' time, to burn all th' books that had caused th' Oldtimes to go wrong. But now . . . I ain't so sure." Louis's eyes were troubled, as if he recalled some long past battle with himself.

"He should have been able to keep th' books," Matthew declared, ever the advocate of the Beforetime.

"I dinna know about that either," Louis said sternly. "Maybe Henry Druid only wanted a look at th' past an' had no mind to seek trouble. Then again, maybe he was after some of th' power th' Oldtimers had."

"You mean th' Beforetimers' magic?" Matthew asked.

"Magic! Pah!" Louis scoffed. "I dinna think for one

moment they was any more magic than us. Not th' sort of magic ye find in fairy stories, anyhow. Some of th' things they could do might seem like magic to us now. But 'tis my feeling they was just mighty clever people—too clever for their own good."

"Well, I think they were magic!" Matthew said stubbornly. "An' I think Lud would never have destroyed them."

That was as close as you could get to outright sedition—and to Louis, who we all agreed was interesting but probably not to be trusted.

But the old man only puffed at his pipe for a minute. "Boy," he said finally. "Ye mun be careful of what ye say. It ain't safe to be blatherin' out every crazy notion. As to what ye said, well, ye could be right. But if ye are, then who made th' Great White? Yer wonderful Beforetimers, that's who."

Matthew's face was stricken, and he did not answer. I remembered that Maruman believed much the same thing.

"However it happened, everything was changed by the Great White," Louis told him, almost gently. "Even th' seasons have changed. Once they were all a similar length. Nothing is like it was in th' Beforetime. The Great White killed th' Beforetime, an' it woke lots of queer things. It ain't th' same world now."

He puffed at his pipe again before continuing. "But maybe th' Beforetimers left some things hidden. Maybe there might be something left, and maybe Henry Druid's books were nowt harmless. Just in case Matthew is right an' th' holocaust were man-made, it might be better to leave that stuff hidden. After all, we dinna want to be finding out how they did it."

"But we wouldn't have to use the magic like they did," Matthew said at last.

Louis shook his head. "Dinna say it, lad. Ye dinna know what ye'd do. Power has a way of . . . changin' a person. In th' end, what would all that power do to yer good intentions?"

From that day on, thoughts of escape began to plague me.

Discovering I was no solitary freak had given rise to the notion that life seemed worth more than just endurance. Obernewtyn hadn't turned out as badly as I had feared, but any way you looked at it, the place was still a prison. And I wanted to be free. I wanted to find Maruman and make a home for us. I imagined a remote farm where we could live quietly with Dameon and Matthew. Cameo, too.

One cloud-filled morning that same week, I was thinking of how useful our abilities might be in throwing off any pursuit, when I was assailed by a premonition of danger as potent as the one I had experienced before Obernewtyn's head keeper had come to the Kinraide orphan home. I had such strong premonitions rarely, and they never revealed much—only that some threat loomed.

Later that day, the promise of rain was fulfilled with a vengeance. The dark skies opened, and the raindrops that fell were big and forceful. Everyone took shelter; those in the orchards ran for the nearest buildings, and even the cows and horses came under cover. I stayed in the shed, milking the cows and listening to the drumming noise the rain made on the tin roof. The disquiet that the premonition had roused gradually faded, and the downpour ended obligingly just before I was due to go back through the maze.

Ariel was waiting at the gate with the others when I arrived, and I was surprised by the air of gloom among them. I thought it was on account of the rain until, when Ariel turned to unlock the maze gate, one of the girls leaned near and whispered, "Madam Vega has returned. Ariel just told us." Her eyes were frightened, and I felt that old fluttery terror come back into my stomach.

It wasn't as if anything had really changed, but all at once I realized what had struck me about the atmosphere at Obernewtyn since I had come here. It had been waiting. . . .

◆ 14 ◆

I HAD THOUGHT I would be summoned by Madam Vega at once. But as the days passed much as before, I wondered whether I could have been wrong about the premonition.

Then I discovered something that drove my nagging worry over the head keeper to the back of my thoughts. Dameon told me he heard Cameo had been receiving "treatments" from the doctor since Madam Vega's return. No one knew precisely what the treatments were, but I remembered the talk at my trial concerning a "cure" for Misfit minds. I found it odd and rather frightening that so little was known of the treatments when Cameo could not have been the first to receive them.

Strangest of all was Cameo's reaction when I asked about her visits to the doctor's chamber. She just stared at me in surprise and said she didn't know what I was talking about. With anyone else, I might have thought they were lying, but not Cameo. She was not made for guile.

Dameon suggested that Cameo and perhaps all those who received the doctor's treatments had been subjected to an Oldtime technique called hypnosis, which could prevent them from remembering what had been done to them. Hypnosis sounded to me like a form of what I called coercion, and I almost said as much. But I had not explained my ability in this area to Dameon or Matthew, fearing they might react uncomfortably to a companion capable of tampering with their minds.

But we agreed, under the circumstances, that I should probe Cameo. To my astonishment, I found a series of blocks at different levels in her mind. They were not natural shields, and I did not see how hypnosis, as Dameon had described it, could have produced them. The worst thing about them was that they were clumsily made and had damaged her mind. This, I thought, might be the reason for both her nightmares and her physical weakening. I suspected I could have forced my way through the blocks, but to do so might hurt Cameo even more.

I withdrew from her, feeling confused and helpless. Most of all, I wondered why her mind had been blocked. What had this Doctor been doing to make him so determined to conceal the nature of his treatments?

It was a week before I saw Cameo again, at a nightmeal. She looked terrible, and Matthew went nearly as white as she was when he saw her enter the dining chamber. He hastened to bring her to join us. When Dameon asked gently where she had been, she would not meet any of our eyes, and said only that she had been ill and resting in a place where they kept sick Misfits. It was impossible to press her any harder. She was clearly happy to see us, and she talked and laughed more as the meal progressed, but there was a brittleness to her behavior, and she had lost a frightening amount of weight.

That night, I had a nightmare. Much as in the dream Cameo had once told me about, I was being pursued through the darkness by something terrible that hungered for me. When I mentioned it to Matthew, he gave me a haunted look and said he had experienced a similar nightmare, only it was not him being pursued but Cameo while he stood by helplessly.

Dameon said nothing, but it was obvious from the shadows under his eyes that he was sleeping badly, too, even if he had not had nightmares. I asked him if his empathy could give us any insight into what was happening.

"I don't perceive others' emotions as clearly as you and Matthew can hear their thoughts. Empathy is much hazier. I can sometimes even project feelings onto another and have tried to send calmness and serenity to Cameo, but her fear is like a wall I cannot surmount."

"Fear of the doctor?" I asked.

"Fear of something. I cannot say what," Dameon said, frowning.

Two nights later, Cameo was moved into my room, an extra bed having been put in to accommodate her. The reasons given were that a new group of Misfits would soon be arriving and extensive repairs were to be carried out in some areas of Obernewtyn before wintertime. Whether this was true or not, I was glad of the opportunity to spend more time with her.

On her first night, I was awakened by her scream. Sitting upright, I stared across at Cameo writhing in her bed. Then I looked in astonishment at the others, who were all still soundly asleep. Finally I realized that I had heard a *mental* scream, which I alone had been capable of receiving. I probed the others lightly to make sure they were truly asleep before getting up and padding across the cold floor.

Cameo was lying with her back to me now, whimpering softly. The moon fell across her pillow. It gleamed whitely in the light, but I could not see her face. She moved sharply and muttered something in an odd, deep voice. It didn't sound like her at all, and the queer thought came to me that it wasn't Cameo lying there, but some other person with soft blond hair.

She moaned and rolled over, and I could see of course it was Cameo. I sagged against the side of her bed, grinning like an idiot at my stupid fright. Then her eyes opened and my grin froze, for the eyes looking out of Cameo's face were the wrong color! They were a hot, sickly ocher hue and full of amusement.

"You'll never find it," she rasped in that same deep, strange voice.

I was petrified, but then I realized she was not actually speaking to me. She was in a trance, and it struck me that I might be able to question her in this state.

"Tell me about the doctor?" I asked softly after checking the others still slept. "What does he do to you?"

"Find it if you can. I'll not show you," said Cameo in the unfamiliar voice. She gave a sneering old woman's cackle of laughter.

I frowned. Her answer made no sense. Looking into her eyes, I wondered with a chill if a demon had taken possession of her. Louis insisted there were no such things, but seeing Cameo transformed like this, I wasn't so sure. All at once, she closed her eyes and dropped into a sound sleep. Returning to my own bed, I had to pinch myself to make sure I hadn't dreamed the whole thing.

"Poor Cameo," Dameon said the next day. "But I do not know what we can do to help her."

"Do you think a sleep drug would help, if we can manage to get some?" I suggested.

Dameon said he did not think sleep drugs were the answer. "She would still dream," he said. "We have to find out *why* she is having so many nightmares and take away whatever is causing them."

That brought us back to the doctor's treatments, but how could we stop them when we did not even know what they were? It occurred to me that night, when Ariel had again led Cameo away, that I could enter his mind. He might not know much, but he would surely know something.

But the next morning, Ariel did not take us to the farms as he usually did. When I asked where he was, one of the girls whispered that three people had tried to escape the previous night, and he was involved in the search. Later I heard the Norselander twins had been captured and were now locked up in cells beneath Obernewtyn. I was not surprised that they had attempted to escape. Had I not heard them plotting to do so? But I wondered who the other person was who had succeeded in getting away, and I hoped he or she would manage it unscathed, for it came to me that the only way to look after Cameo might be for us to escape with her.

Dameon and Matthew were as interested as I was in

the identity of the escaped Misfit, and we spent mid-meal and nightmeal that day speculating on who it might be.

Afterward, when I returned to my room, I found Cameo alone, sitting on her bed. Going to sit beside her, I asked her gently where she had been the previous night. She lifted her head as if it were too heavy for the slender stalk of her neck and said dully that she had been ill. I asked who had been treating her, but she only shrugged, though it seemed to me the shrug was as much a shudder as anything else. Then she burst into tears, and holding her, it occurred to me that sooner or later, her mind would crumble under the pressure of what was being done to her.

"I'm so scared," she whispered suddenly, turning her tear-stained face to me. "It didn't seem so awful at all when I came here. Not like I expected it to be. But now I keep dreaming of things chasing me and of an old lady laughing." That sounded like the persona that I had seen during her trance, and I wondered if the blocks were beginning to break down. I debated whether to press her but decided against it, because she looked so ill and exhausted.

The next morning, at firstmeal, I heard someone ask if Selmar had been caught. She had been missing from her bed for more than a week, and I had assumed she had been moved to another room or had been wandering at night as she had been wont to do.

"Caught?" I asked.

"Haven't you heard?" said the girl beside me. "She was with the twins when they tried to escape, but she got away."

It had never occurred to me that a defective might

be the unknown escaped Misfit. Astonished at this news, it was a moment before I turned to Cameo, who had come to the meal with me. Her face had gone the color of dirty soap, and I wondered why the news that Selmar had escaped Obernewtyn provoked such a look of horror. Looking down at my food, I remembered suddenly what Louis Larkin had said about Selmar being different when she first came to Obernewtyn, and a terrible idea formed in my mind. What if the thing that had turned Selmar into a defective was the doctor's treatments? I was suddenly determined to question Louis about Selmar, and if he would not answer me willingly, then I would enter his mind and find out for myself what had happened to her.

I was shocked when Louis flew into a rage the moment I mentioned Selmar's name. He ordered me out of the milking barn, so there was no opportunity to probe him. I had simply to slink away, wondering why he reacted so violently. Only later did it occur to me that he had done so because he knew Selmar had escaped and feared for her. Hadn't there been real fondness in his voice when he had mentioned her before? Perhaps before she had become defective, they had been friends.

That night, no one knew whether or not Selmar had been caught, but there was a rumor that the twins were being sent to one of the remote Councilfarms that dealt with the cleansing of whitestick. It was no less of a death sentence that if they had been ordered burnt.

Ariel's absence continued, and more than once I heard it whispered that he was not just involved in the search for Selmar but was leading it. One boy told me that Ariel and his dogs—wolves, really—always chased anyone who ran off. And he always caught them.

Remembering Selmar's reaction to Ariel, I pitied her, though I could hardly credit that he would use wolves to hunt her, for it was said that, unlike dogs, they would not be stayed from a kill.

I decided I would definitely deep-probe Ariel when he next showed himself. I would have tried again with Louis Larkin, but when Rushton came for us at the maze gate the next day, he said coolly that I had offended the old man and he had refused to have me in the milking barn. Therefore I would be mucking out stables that day. Rushton seemed to relish giving me the reassignment, and a cold anger filled me. I decided I would probe him instead. He might only be the farm overseer, but as such he might know something about the hunt for Selmar if dogs were used.

Then I thought of Sharna, and my heart quickened, for he might know something of these dogs Ariel was supposed to be using. But Sharna was not in the stables, and Rushton did not linger, so in a moment, I was alone. Even the horses had already been led out. In spite of everything, it was delicious to be entirely alone, and I lowered my shield and loosened my thoughts to let them fly and hover. It felt odd, since I had not done this since I was a child in Rangorn, and only ever when I was alone, roaming in the fields and on the edge of the forest, for to send out my thoughts in this way meant my body would remain motionless as a doll until I returned to it.

I felt almost light-headed as my mind floated free of my body; waves of thought and impressions washed over me. They came from every corner of the stable, flitting like butterflies, drifting like peat smoke. Idle thoughts about how to saddle a horse that had never been ridden or what to do with a fevered mare, a fleeting thought about a bitter wintertime when hundreds of animals had died. The barn was alive with memories now that I had opened myself to receive the imprints they had made. There was no telling how long the impression of a thought might last. It depended on the thinker and the time and the place and a dozen other things.

Remembering my intention to probe Rushton, I raised his image in my thoughts, seeking his mind in particular. The beauty of probing him at a distance was that even if he felt something, he would not associate it with me. But I would be very careful and reach only into the upper levels of his mind.

I pushed my thoughts farther afield, striving out to where Misfits were picking fruit, and beyond to where livestock grazed in far fields, into every corner of the farms. I was ranging too widely now to receive any individual thoughts; it was like traveling through a pool and getting deeper and deeper without ever touching the bottom.

I went out beyond Obernewtyn, forgetting Rushton for the moment and wondering how far I could go. If it was possible to go beyond the mountains, I might be able to reach Maruman. But before I could try, something brushed against my mind.

I recoiled, but curiosity made me withdraw only a little way. Foolishly, I ventured near again, and again my thoughts touched something. It was not a mind but some sort of force. I touched it again and felt it squirm. Then it reached out and enveloped me. Suddenly I was afraid. I began to withdraw, but the force grew stronger and held me tightly. Frantically, I pulled back, but whatever the force was that I had disturbed began to drive me back toward my own body. I fought, but I was like a leaf in a storm. I became aware of the nearness of my body. Dimly I registered that I had fallen to my knees.

Inexorably, I was forced into my body, and to my horror, it was my body as well as my mind that was now trapped. I could not move a muscle! A drumming sounded in my ears, and a wave of new fright washed over me when I realized that the force was summoning my body.

With a sob, I felt my legs tremble. Against my will, I began to walk stiffly toward the open door of the stable.

"No!" I screamed, but inwardly, since not even my mouth would respond to my will.

Then I sensed another mind. It was not like the mindless force that had taken hold of me. It was human, but there was something strange about it, too. But any curiosity I might have felt was swamped by my terror.

"O reaching girlmind . . . who?"

This other mind was far stronger than Matthew's, but there was something disjointed about it, as if a voice spoke in an echoing chamber. I felt the cool touch of the other mind, and its tendrils meshed gently with mine. Instinctively, I fought free of its embrace, knowing that such a connection would reveal me utterly to that unknown mind. Yet in that moment I had sensed its desire to help me.

"Who are you?" I asked.

"Trust me, sistermind. What is your name? My friends and I have sensed you before."

I struggled for a moment in the viselike grip of the

inhuman force and realized I was about to walk out into the open.

"Help me!" I cried to the other.

"Perhaps if we help, you will trust. You are strong. But the machine that holds you is too strong for you to fight. Together we will be stronger. Meld with me, and when I signal, pull away as hard as you can. The machine has no mind to make a decision. It will not realize that to divide is to conquer."

"I can't meld," I said desperately, fearing the revelation that would result almost as much as I feared the terrible force that held my mind and drew my body forward.

"You must," said the othermind urgently.

I was in the doorway now, and I was suddenly fearful that whoever controlled the force that had taken hold of me was determined to make me reveal who I was. Terror gave me strength, and I swayed uncertainly, neither moving forward nor back as I battled the force with every bit of strength I could muster.

It was not enough. I stepped out into the sunlight.

"I will meld," I agreed in desperation. The othermind moved forward at once, and I felt a great desire to simply surrender to those soft tendrils. But as if it knew my fear of a deeper melding, the othermind held itself rigidly away from the center of my thoughts.

"Now!" it called, and we began a terrific tug-of-war. As predicted, the machine, if such it was, tried to keep us both but did not have the strength. The moment it slid off me, I slammed a shield into place.

I staggered back inside the stables, appalled to discover the extent of my weakness. My face dripped with perspiration, and I wiped it hastily on my sleeve.

A machine able to exert a force that could capture a mind! I was astounded and frightened, and not only because someone was apparently using a forbidden Beforetime device. It was the knowledge that whoever was using it might know about people like Matthew and me. And so, I thought, must the Oldtimers who had created such a machine. But I dismissed that notion. My abilities, like Matthew's and Dameon's, were Misfit abilities that had arisen from the poisons of the Great White.

My more immediate concern was the identity of the strange othermind that had helped me.

There was nothing to do but to get on with mucking out the stables, and I did so slowly, because the battle with the machine had drained me. I cursed the stupidity that had led me to farseek. I would not dare attempt it again. In fact, I was now too frightened to use any but the most basic powers, for perhaps any use of my abilities would draw that malevolent force to me again. And the othermind might not be there to rescue me a second time.

My vague notion of escape grew into a determination to get away from Obernewtyn and all of its mysteries and dangers. Cameo must come, and Dameon and Matthew. I knew of no other I cared to trust. Fleetingly, I thought of my rescuer. A man, I thought, but there was no way to contact him without arousing the machine. Anyway, he seemed smart and strong enough to take care of himself, and he had spoken of friends, so he was not alone.

Learning what had happened over midmeal, and agog with delight to hear of the othermind, Matthew disagreed. "If we really are going to escape, yer bound to take him an' his friends, too. After all, he saved ye."

"There is no way to learn who they are with that machine ready to catch any probe," I said.

"There must be some way," he insisted, entranced with the idea of my gallant rescuer.

I was less romantic. "He might not even want to leave. We don't know if he is a Misfit or if he is at Obernewtyn. I'm not even really sure it's a he. And the whole thing might have been a trap."

"Ungrateful Elspethelf," Matthew sputtered into thought.

"He helped me, and I am grateful he saved my life," I conceded hastily, forestalling one of Matthew's emotive lectures. "Which is why I am not going to throw it away trying to learn who he is. That would be truly ungrateful."

"Speaking of help," Dameon interjected quietly, "I have been thinking. If you really intend to escape, you should not take me. I would slow you down. And it is not so bad for me here."

"Of course yer comin' with us!" Matthew said firmly. "We've taken yer blindness into account."

Dameon smiled at his friend sadly. "Sometimes I think you have more heart than sense. Most times," he corrected comically, and we all laughed. Then Dameon grew serious again. "Well, if I am to come, then I will speak. This is a dead quest from the start if it is not planned carefully. Have you thought what will happen if we *do* get away? We have no Certificates, and we will stand out wherever we go."

I stared at him. I had not thought beyond escape,

but he was right. We had to plan everything, otherwise we would find ourselves condemned to whitestick cleansing.

"What about dressing up as gypsies?" Dameon said.

"Wonderful!" I cried, for gypsies did not have Normalcy Certificates, and they were nomads that moved constantly about the Land.

Suddenly Matthew stiffened, looking over my shoulder. "Look out. It is our surly friend, the overseer." I turned my head slightly to see that he was talking with another Misfit.

"He takes an interest in us," Dameon said softly, obviously empathising the overseer as he came closer. "He does not like what he sees."

"Maybe he's only interested in one of us," Matthew muttered with a sly glance in my direction.

Catching the gist of his thoughts, I scowled. "Don't be an idiot," I snapped. Rushton made no pretense of his dislike of me.

"He's coming over," Matthew said, and we all munched our food casually.

"You! Elspeth. I have a job for you," Rushton called. Nodding to the others, I got to my feet and went to the waiting overseer. I could not make out his expression, because the sun was behind him. He led me away.

"You are foolish to make your friendships so blatant," he said angrily. I stared at him in astonishment. "But I did not call you to say that. The girl Selmar sleeps in your chamber. When did you last see her?"

"She wanders at night," I said, suspicious at his knowledge of household matters.

"Did she sleep there the night before she disappeared?" he queried.

"I don't know. I don't know when she disappeared, I mean," I said, completely dumbfounded. "Why do you want to know?"

"You have no right to ask me questions," he said haughtily.

I saw red. "And what right have you to ask them of me?"

"I belong here," he said icily. I did not dare speak; he was so angry. "Fool of a girl," he snarled. "Go back to your cows."

Bewildered by the encounter, I went to the barn. Louis was waiting, and he seemed to have forgotten his anger with me. Recklessly, I asked him again about Selmar.

To my surprise, he did not lose his temper, but only sighed. "She were a lovely girl," he said sadly. I frowned, because he was talking as if she were dead.

"She is free," I said gently, now certain that they had once been friends.

"No," he responded, anguish in his face. "That devil-spawned brat, Ariel, has caught her, and no doubt he has taken her to the doctor, though what more he can do to the poor bairn, I dinna ken."

"That is what happened to Selmar, isn't it?" I asked slowly. "The doctor's treatments destroyed her mind."

"He never meant it to be so here, th' first master didn't," Louis said. I did not understand what he meant, but instinct kept me silent as he went on. "He were a good man, an' he built this place because he thought th' mountain air were a healin' thing. Two sons an' a wife he had buried already from the rotting sickness, an' another child burned. He wanted to make this place a sanctuary, and he took another wife to help him in his work. But she were no helpmate, an' when he died, their son, Michael, were too weak to fight against the yellow-eyed vixen. It was she that started buyin' Misfits from the Council."

I wanted to ask about the doctor, but Louis set me to churning, so instead I thought about the things he had told me. The first Master of Obernewtyn—Lukas Seraphim—had moved here out of grief and a desire to start anew. He had married again—someone Louis called a "yellow-eyed vixen," who must be the mother of Michael Seraphim, who had grown up to become the second Master of Obernewtyn. Though from what Louis said, his mother had been the true master. But who was master now?

That evening, on my way back from the farms, one thought overshadowed all these others. Louis had confirmed my fear that the doctor's treatments could leave Cameo a ruin. It seemed to me that the only way to save her would be to make our escape, and soon.

I meant to speak to the others about it at nightmeal, but I had not long sat down before someone came to tell me the doctor wished to interview me the next day.

✦ 15 ✦

I woke early the next morning, feeling as if I had slept badly, though I could not remember any nightmare. Our rooms were always unlocked in the morning by one of the Misfits, and it was the only time we could really do as we pleased. Most mornings I readied myself for the day slowly, but today I was too apprehensive. I dressed swiftly and went straightaway to the kitchen. I was pleased to find Matthew had got there before me. He asked me about Cameo, and I had to shake my head and admit that she had not slept in her bed the night before.

We talked about what I had learned from Louis Larkin. Matthew was more worried than ever when I told him my theory that Selmar had been rendered defective by the doctor's treatments. He suggested that we talk seriously about escape at midmeal.

I swallowed and finally forced myself to tell him that I would not be going to the farms that morning because the doctor had summoned me.

He looked aghast. "Do ye know Louis once warned me to watch out for him? He said there was a dragon in the doctor's chamber. What does that mean, I'd like to know?"

"I hope I don't find out," I said.

The outside door opened with a gust of wind and a bang that made everyone including the cook turn and look to see who had come in. It was only a Misfit named Willie, whom Matthew nicknamed Sly Willie because he was a known informer. But just behind him came an older man who was a stranger. He was not a Guardian or a Councilman, but his clothes were so faded that it was impossible to tell if he wore the green of a traveling jack or the brown motley of a potmender. He must be one or the other, I thought. Who else would make the long, hard journey up to Obernewtyn?

"Who is that?" Matthew whispered.

I shrugged, but something about the stranger seemed familiar. He sat down at a table near us, and Andra gave him something to eat. He was very tall and tanned, and the knees of his pants were sturdily patched. He ate, shoveling the food down as Willie sat opposite him.

"So where do ye come from?" Willie asked.

"From the Lowlands," the man grunted. "I had to cross badlands on foot. No one warned me that pass is tainted like it is."

"As long as you kept to the path and didn't stop, you won't have been hurt," Willie said. "We don't get many visitors," he added

The stranger shrugged. "I came up because I heard there might be work for me. Potmetal is my specialty."

Hearing this, Andra came forward to speak with him. Most of the kitchen pots were in need of repair, and the potmender said he would do as much as he could that day and the next. The man spread out his tools to work, and the cook cuffed Willie and sent him about his business.

I had been told to wait in the kitchen after firstmeal when the others left to go down to the farms. I had thought Andra might decide to put me to work, but she did not, and so I watched the potmender at his craft. I was more convinced than ever that I had seen him somewhere before, but I could not remember where.

Then Sly Willie appeared again and, leering, bid me come with him to see the doctor and Madam Vega.

My mouth went dry, but I refused to let the informant see my fear as I followed him wordlessly from the kitchen and into a part of Obernewtyn I had not seen since the night of my arrival.

We passed through the entrance to Obernewtyn and into a windowless hall lit by pale green candles, which flickered and hissed as we passed. At the end of the hall was a small room with a single bench seat. Here, Willie told me to wait. My legs shook so much that I sat down and tried to make myself calm. I remembered all too well what had come of the last interview with Madam Vega, when I had let fear get the better of me. This time, I was determined to remain in control. If the woman did have some sort of sensitivity to Misfit abilities like mine, I must make sure I did not let her provoke me into using them. That way she might come to doubt her assessment that I was a birth Misfit and decide not to bother sending me to the doctor.

It was a slim hope, but I clung to it. I had one moment in which to wonder where the real Master of Obernewtyn was, and to think he was no less mysterious than the doctor, when Willie emerged from a door and gestured for me to go through. There was a sulkiness in his face that made me think he had wanted to stay while I was being interviewed and had been sent away. Willie was one of those informants who served his masters out of spite and slyness rather than out of fear or for favor.

Taking a deep breath outside the door, I pushed it open resolutely and reminded myself to stay calm no matter what happened. My first impression on entering was of heat. A quick look around revealed the source— a fire burning brightly in an open fireplace despite the warmth of the weather. Spare wood was piled high on one side of the fire, and two comfortable-looking armchairs were drawn up facing the hearth. The stone floor was covered by a brightly colored woven rug, and there were a number of attractive tapestries hanging on the walls. It was a pleasant, lavish room compared to the rest of Obernewtyn.

Against the back wall of the room was a desk, and behind this a wide window with a magnificent view of the cold arching sky and the jagged mountains. I stared, mesmerized, until Madam Vega stepped abruptly into my line of sight, the same stylishly attractive figure that I remembered. But her expression was no longer the coy, girlish one she had worn during her visit at Kinraide. Her blue eyes were cold and calculating, and she waved me impatiently to the chair nearest the fire. I sat down obediently, though a strange smell seemed to emanate from the fireplace, and I felt slightly sickened by it.

"You should have told me that you had only begun to show Misfit tendencies after being exposed to tainted water," Madame Vega said briskly. "I thought . . ." She bit off the words and drew a long breath.

"Still," she said after a moment, her voice now calm. "There may be some use in you. I am told that you have formed a circle of friends." I opened my mouth to deny it, but she held up her hand to silence me. "Do not trouble to lie. It bores me, and you do not want to bore me." There was a clear threat in her words, and I swallowed and said nothing.

"Well then," she said sweetly. She sat back in her seat and watched me through narrowed eyes. "Tell me about your friends," she said.

I thought of Rushton and damned him. It seemed he was an informer after all. "I only eat with them at meals," I said. "I won't do it again."

Irritation flicked over her features. "There is nothing wrong in your forming friendships. Indeed, it will suit me if you widen your group of friends. You will be my eyes and ears among the Misfits."

I stared. "I couldn't spy," I said stiffly. I would pretend stupidity but not that.

"I do not want you to report plots and petty misdeeds or even subversive gossip," she said so kindly that I was filled with suspicion. "All I want you to do is watch for any Misfits who seem . . . different. I am concerned that some of those brought here do not reveal the full extent of their . . . mutancy. That is most unfortunate, because it means we cannot help them." She performed this beautifully, and I even saw a hint of tears in her eyes. But I could only think of what was being done to Cameo. And what had been done to Selmar.

"What do you mean by different?" I asked, hoping I sounded dull-witted rather than frightened.

"I want to know of anyone with unusual or undisclosed deviations of the mind," she said. I could do no more than nod. "Good. I am sure you will be of much help to me," she purred. She smoothed her skirt and said very casually, "Cameo tells me you are her friend."

I felt the snakelike coil of fear in my belly. "She is a defective true dreamer," I said, but I wondered how much Cameo had said when she was hypnotized. We had not spoken to her about our undisclosed abilities, but neither had we been careful not to refer to them in front of her. Was it possible that she had said something that had made Madam Vega want to look more closely at our group?

"She behaves as if she were defective, but that is something that can be made to seem so, rather than being so. And even true dreams may be a pretense." She said the last word with a coy, almost teasing smile that invited me to share the joke.

"I do not think she is pretending," I said stolidly, determined to make her think of me as a dullard.

"Very well," she said with sudden impatience. "I am going to take you to the doctor's chamber now. Get up," she added, coming toward me, her satin dress whispering to the rug. I rose, and she came to stand behind me. She stood so close that I felt her breath stir my hair. A moment of blind terror made me want to turn where I could see her, but I forced myself to be still.

"Come," she said at last, but she seemed to be gesturing to the fireplace. I went closer, only then seeing that one of the panels alongside the fireplace was an ornate door, so intricately worked in carving to match the panels on either side of it that I had not even noticed it was there. Opened, it led into a narrow hall, which smelled of damp. There was another door at the end of the short hall, and when Madam Vega opened it, a great wave of heat rushed out.

"The doctor's chamber," Madam Vega murmured, though she seemed to say this more to herself than to me. Despite its secretive entrance, it was an enormous circular room. There were no windows, but light flooded in from a huge skylight in the center of the ceiling. A fireplace almost as big as the one in the kitchen provided the nearly unbearable heat, but I paid less attention to this than I might have done, for there were books everywhere, not only those of recent origin—easily recognizable by their coarse workmanship and the purple Council stamp of approval—but also hundreds of smaller, beautifully made books that could only have been made in the Beforetime. Forbidden books, I thought, gazing around with amazement at walls lined with bookshelves, each full to overflowing. There were tables everywhere, and these, too, were piled with books as well as loose papers and maps.

"Doctor Seraphim?" called Madam Vega.

I was trying to understand what this name could mean, for surely Seraphim was the name of the Master of Obernewtyn, when there was a flurry of movement, and a rotund man emerged smiling from a dim corner. If this was the mysterious and sinister doctor responsible for what had happened to Selmar, his appearance was utterly unexpected. He greeted Madam Vega and drew up two chairs to the sweltering mouth of the fire. He bid us sit, and Madame Vega gestured to me to obey, but she remained standing. The doctor sat in the other chair and beamed at me.

"Another Misfit," he sighed, leaning over to peer nearsightedly into my face. Then he giggled suddenly and slapped his leg as if I had made a joke. It was a high-pitched, almost hysterical laugh, and I thought again that this could not really be the terrible and powerful doctor I had been so frightened of meeting.

"You are a cool one," he gurgled coyly, wagging his finger at me. I did not know what to say, and I glanced helplessly at Madam Vega, but she was gazing around the room with a distracted air. Without warning, she moved away purposefully between the shelves, leaving me alone with the doctor.

"You don't look like a Misfit," he said, peering at me closely again. "Vega tells me you are a dreamer and that tainted water caused your dreams, but the reports that came with you make me suspect that your exposure to tainted water only served to rouse latent Misfit tendencies. I am interested in the idea that such exposure could be used to increase certain Misfit traits so that they could be more easily studied."

I said nothing, and indeed he seemed to be speaking to himself rather than to me. He sighed and shrugged. "Unfortunately, I do not have the time right now to begin a new research project. I have several important experiments to complete, and they will require all of my attention. However, I am going to write your name down for future research." He gave the same wide, encouraging smile, as if this news ought to please me, and then he got up and began rummaging through the contents on a cluttered table.

I glanced around, wondering where Madam Vega had gone. I noticed an enormous and very fine portrait of a woman hanging in a small alcove. I felt instantly repelled by the painted face, which seemed cruel and cold to me.

"I see you are looking at my dear grandmama," said the doctor. He gazed at the painting for a long moment, and several emotions flickered over his face: fear, awe, confusion. "Her name was Marisa," he whispered.

I saw the chance to ingratiate myself. "She is beautiful," I said admiringly, though I thought the face too sharp and cold for beauty. But she was handsome, and there was a fiery gleaming intelligence in the eyes. Yellow eyes, I noticed.

"She *was* beautiful," said the doctor. "It was such a shame she had to die."

This was such an odd thing to say that I turned to look at him, but the doctor had discovered a pencil at last. "Elspeth Gordie, wasn't it?"

I nodded, and he bent over a scrap of parchment and scribed laboriously, muttering, "Misfits are not always what they appear to be, you know. Often there are more demons that the treatment reveals. Do you know I once treated a girl who harbored amazing demons? Selmar was her name. Once I had forced the demons to reveal themselves, I was able to offer treatments that rendered her quite docile in the end. Presently, I am treating another who may be hiding demons."

The only demons you find in people's minds are the ones you put there with your treatments, I thought, all amusement at his foolish smile and dithering manner swallowed up in a surge of outrage at the knowledge that he was talking about Cameo. I looked at my feet, afraid the cold hatred of my heart would show in my eyes.

"Doctor, I do not think you should discuss such matters with a Misfit," said a voice as rich and smooth as undiluted honey.

"Alexi," said the doctor, looking over my shoulder with a flustered, almost guilty expression. I turned slowly and there stood a tall, beautiful man with shining white hair. His skin was pale and soft like that of a child, and his eyes were the coldest and darkest I had ever seen. As he stepped closer, I stood up, fighting an over-powering urge to back away.

"Of course, you're right. I was forgetting," said the doctor, talking too quickly, getting to his feet as well. He seemed afraid of the other man. Alexi flicked his unsettling eyes over me.

"Alexi is my assistant," the doctor said, and I fought the impulse to gape. "Would you like to examine her, Alexi? The tainted water may have acted as a catalyst—"

"I am sick of this," Alexi snarled, cutting the doctor off. "I have no use for yet another dreamer. Get rid of her. Where is Vega?" he asked imperiously.

The doctor looked around vaguely. "She was here . . . a moment ago," he said.

The other man turned his shadow-dark eyes on me. The irises seemed to be much larger than usual, with very little white visible around them. "Well, sit down. I might as well see if there is any use in you."

I sat down again, and Alexi sat in the chair vacated by the doctor.

"Her name is Elspeth," bleated the doctor, hovering nervously behind him.

Alexi ignored him and fixed me in his frigid black stare. "Your family were seditioners?" he asked.

I did not know if he was asking or telling me, so I nodded slightly.

"They were burned by the Herders?"

I nodded again, aware that he must have read my record, too.

"You dream true?" he asked.

"Sometimes," I said, but my voice came out as a croak.

"Are you able to know what people feel or think before they tell you?" he asked.

My heart almost stopped, but I managed to shake my head.

"Can you sometimes sense things that have happened before, in rooms or . . . or from an object?"

I shook my head again.

"What was the crime of your parents?" he asked. "For what were they charged?"

"Sedition," I said.

Without warning, he leapt to his feet, knocking the chair he had been sitting in to the ground with a great clatter. "She is useless. When will the right one be found?" he snarled.

"The blond girl . . . ," the doctor quavered, but Alexi shut him up with a poisonous look.

"My dear Alexi," said Madam Vega, emerging from behind some of the shelves. "I have been looking for you."

Alexi stalked over to her. "This one is impossibly stupid. I have enough idiocy to endure without your bringing me another fool. Why did you bring her here?"

"I already told you what happened. And she is here now because Stephen wanted to see her," Madam Vega said in a soft but steely voice, nodding toward the doctor.

It was all I could do to stop myself from gaping at the doctor, who hovered nearby, smiling too much and wringing his hands anxiously as he watched his so-called assistant rage. For Stephen Seraphim *was* the name of the current Master of Obernewtyn. But how could this ineffectual young man be legal master of anything?

"Does it not occur to you that stupidity is easily feigned?" Madame Vega was saying to Alexi now. "The one we seek would be clever enough to pretend stupidity or that she is no more than a dreamer and a defective. Have a care, someday you will make a fatal error in your impatience."

"Are you trying to tell me this creature is the one we are looking for?" Alexi snapped.

"Of course not. I have told you this one was a mistake, but there are others that might seem no less foolish," she added calmly.

"This last fiasco—" Alexi began, but Vega soothed him.

"We will speak of that matter later," she said, her eyes sliding pointedly to where I sat. She moved closer to me, her expression vaguely threatening. She studied me speculatively for a moment, and then crooked a finger at me. She waited until I had risen, then grasped my chin in hard, cold fingers.

"It is not wise to speak of this visit to the doctor, Elspeth. You will be most regretful if I hear that you have gossiped of this visit. Indeed, it would be better if you forgot altogether." She stared hard into my eyes, and for a moment her mind seemed to brush against mine. I was shocked to realize that she was not just sensitive to Misfit powers like mine—she possessed a small ability herself. Though probably unaware of her power, it was what made her such a good hunter of Misfits.

I managed to keep my face bland. Finally, she released my chin and said, "In the meantime, remember what I have said about your friends." I felt a chill at the underlying menace of her tone and did not doubt for one moment that she would carry out the implied threat.

Returning with Sly Willie to work in the kitchens for the remainder of the day, I understood the reason that people were prevented from speaking about their visits to the doctor. It wasn't to hide the truth about his treatments. It was to ensure no one knew that control of Obernewtyn had fallen to Madam Vega and Alexi.

✦ 16 ✦

THE NEXT MORNING dawned warm and fair, but I woke with the memory of the previous day lodged inside my mind like an icicle radiating coldness. I dressed hastily and went to the kitchen, but before I could begin to tell Matthew anything of what had happened with the doctor, he told me Ariel had returned.

"Selmar?" I asked, thinking of what Louis had said.

He shook his head, saying there was still no sign of her. I noticed several people seated close were listening avidly to us, and I decided to save my own news until midmeal on the farms, where we could ensure that we would not be overheard. It had occurred to me the night before that I was unlikely to be the only person Madam Vega had set to spy.

In the fields that morning, we all toiled hard, bringing in the harvest. Every spare Misfit was on the farms now, and each of the sections was alive with activity. To my delight, later in the morning Matthew and I were among those sent out to bale a field of hay. Baling was a two-person job, and whenever we were at the end of our row, we were far enough from the other teams to be able to talk.

"Where is Dameon?" I asked, for although he had come to the farms with us, I had not seen him since.

"He was assigned to th' dryin' rooms," Matthew said. "We're spread too thin over too many jobs. It was like this last year, too. It seems like a big fuss, but wintertime is really a killer in the mountains. Ye ken that stranger that Sly Willie brought to th' kitchen yesterday? Well, I saw him talking to Rushton later in th' day," Matthew said.

I scowled, certain the overseer had reported our friendship to Madam Vega. On the other hand, it seemed likely to me that his conversation with the stranger had only concerned the broken plow I had heard him mention to Louis some days before. I said so to Matthew, who looked disappointed. I could not help but think crossly that there were more than enough mysteries and plots at Obernewtyn without longing for more.

"So what happened in th' doctor's chamber, or don't you remember?" Matthew asked at last.

I drew a deep breath and told Matthew that I had only been questioned. "The doctor is too busy to be bothered with me at the moment, but he plans to get back to me later." I glanced around to make sure no one had come close enough to hear us, adding, "Madam Vega made it very clear that there would be unpleasant consequences if I talked about my visit. I think that must be how they shut up people who only go there once. As for those the doctor treats, well, maybe Dameon is right about hypnosis." In fact, I was no longer convinced hypnosis had been used on anyone. Madam Vega had told me to forget about my visit to the doctor, at the same time exerting her coercive ability. A normal person given that command would simply obey her and forget, but my own abilities had deflected her. I could not speak about any of this to Matthew without mentioning my own talent in this area. I would eventually do so, I promised myself, but not yet.

"What else happened?" Matthew urged.

"Madam Vega asked me to keep a watch for Misfits who were unusual."

Matthew paled. "Us?" he gasped.

"People like us. I'm sure she didn't suspect me. My being here is a mistake according to her. The doctor only wanted to see me because they believe my tainted-water ruse, and he was curious about the effect of the accident."

Matthew laughed incredulously. "What is he like?" he asked.

I frowned. "He is defective," I said. "And he is the Master of Obernewtyn."

Matthew stopped working and gave me a look of disbelief. "He can't be. It's against Council lore fer a defective to inherit."

"Exactly why they wouldn't want us talking about our visits to him," I whispered fiercely.

"But . . . then who is runnin' Obernewtyn?" Matthew asked.

"Madam Vega and . . ." I stopped, uncertain of the relationship between Alexi and Madam Vega. And she was careful to humor the doctor. Clearly she did not want to alienate him.

"Madam Vega an' who?" Matthew prompted impatiently.

I swallowed. "There was an older man in the doctor's chamber, called Alexi. The doctor—Stephen Seraphim—called him his assistant, but he didn't act like anyone's assistant. He acted like he was the master and he could barely be bothered with the doctor. Madam Vega fussed over him as if he was important. I think they are in league, and they keep the doctor as a sort of tame pet."

"But what about the treatments?" Matthew asked. "Surely a defective . . ."

"The doctor spoke of treating Cameo, and from what he said, he treated Selmar, too. But Alexi talked as if he was involved as well."

"Maybe they are both treating her in different ways," Matthew said. We fell silent as we passed another baling team.

I thought of the questions Alexi had asked me before losing his temper. Then I thought of Madam Vega instructing me to keep watch for Misfits that were more than they seemed, and a chill ran through me. "Matthew, what if they thought Cameo was like us and hiding it?"

"But why would they care?" Matthew asked. He gave me a quick warning look, and another couple passed behind us. When they were out of earshot, he leaned close and said softly, "We have to get away from here." I knew he was thinking of Cameo, and nodded.

The bell for midmeal rang, and I joined Dameon while Matthew went to stand in line for our food. I had time to tell the empath what had happened the previous day before Matthew returned, practically stuttering with excitement. "Ye'll never guess!" he cried. "Selmar is back! Sly Willie told me Ariel brought her back. He says a new Misfit has arrived, too."

"Was he telling the truth?" I asked cautiously.

"Oh yes, I think so. He said she was defective by mischance, and the Councilmen want her healed."

"Selmar?" I asked, puzzled.

Matthew shook his head. "The new Misfit."

"I meant was he telling the truth about Selmar?" I asked patiently.

"No gain in him lying," Matthew said.

I noticed Cameo standing in the shadow by the maze wall, watching us. "Where have you come from?" I asked her gently, bringing her over to sit down. She did not answer, and when I saw her eyes I realized she was in some sort of trance.

"Something terrible is going to happen," she whispered. She looked straight into my eyes. "They are looking for you. They want you. They want your power. . . ." She slumped forward in a dead faint.

"Oh, Cam," Matthew whispered, and gathered her up into his arms.

I stared at them, my mind whirling.

"She is delirious," Dameon tried to assure me. "She does not know what she is saying."

But it was hard to believe it was a coincidence. Madame Vega had talked about looking for someone, and now Cameo said someone was looking for me. Suddenly I remembered that Maruman had talked of something waiting for me in the mountains.

Dameon shuddered violently.

"I'm sorry," I said, quelling the ripples of fear that ran down my spine.

Dameon looked pale. "It cannot be helped. You are in danger?"

"I think we are all in danger," I said. "They're looking for people like us."

Dameon's face took on a determined look. "Then we must get away from here before it is too late."

"What about Cameo?" Matthew asked.

148

"Cameo will recover, if we get her away," Dameon said decisively. "There is no time to lose. We must make our plans and act swiftly, lest we be trapped by the winter, for the pass to the lowlands is closed by the first blizzards and remains impassible until spring."

"We need to know more about the mountains, because we can't make straight for the lowland pass after we get away," I said. "It would be too obvious, and we would be captured even before we reached it." I told them about the maps I had seen in the doctor's chamber. "If we had a map of the area, there might even be another pass through the mountains that would keep us off the main road."

"Who will lead us if yer caught stealin' into the doctor's chamber?" Matthew interjected.

"There are those made to lead and those to follow," I said slowly. "And there are those who walk a lone path, to scout the way ahead. I am a scout at heart. We need someone smart and steady and wise to be our leader. Dameon would be my choice."

"But I am blind," Dameon said, visibly astonished.

"You are not blind when true seeing is wanted," I said. "You will lead us with those cautious instincts of yours and not be led astray by false paths."

"Oh, wise and tricky Elspethelf," Matthew laughed. Cameo stirred in his arms, and he looked down at her with quick concern until she settled. Then he looked from me to Dameon, his expression sober. "Ye know I'd follow either of ye, so maybe I am a follower. But if Dameon is leader an' says ye mun nowt go to th' doctor's chamber, ye mun obey him."

"Well?" I asked Dameon, somewhat defiantly.

Dameon shook his head slowly. "I will accept the

role of leader for now, but I wish you had not given me the power of veto, Matthew, for I must disappoint you. If Elspeth can find a map, it would be worth some risk. Also, you might look out for an arrowcase. Do you know what that is?"

I nodded. "A thing of metal to point the direction," I said. "My father said the Beforetimers called it a compass."

"No good will come of this," Matthew said darkly as Cameo woke. She struggled from his arms and stood up, seemingly unaware of her collapse or her words prior to that.

Matthew watched her go sadly.

I worked alone that afternoon, cleaning and oiling bridles and saddles and other equipment for storage. I was glad of the time alone to think. No wonder there were so few permanent guardians, and temporary guardians were not permitted to stay at the main house. No wonder official visitors were discouraged. I wondered suddenly what would happen if a visiting party of Councilmen from the lowlands did come up to Obernewtyn unannounced, for they rarely traveled without an escort of soldierguards. Was that why Madam Vega kept Stephen Seraphim content? So he could be brought out at need? In a brief and artfully handled interview, his defective mind might not be apparent.

By the time I went to the evening meal, I had made up my mind to go to the doctor's chamber that very night.

Then I saw Selmar.

Ariel led her into the kitchens. She moved like a

puppet, and when Ariel went away from her, she sat without moving. Her face was bloodless. Even her lips were white, and her eyes stared blankly ahead as if she was as blind as Dameon. But unlike the empath, her face was empty of all expression. She was like a body without a mind.

Cameo was sitting at the same table as Selmar, and her eyes were fixed on the older girl. She looked terrified.

◆ 17 ◆

THE HALLS WERE chill and silent as I slipped along them in stocking feet. I encountered many closed doors, but their locks were simple enough to require very little power, and I did not let myself become discouraged by the amount of time it was taking me to get to the doctor's chamber. The sight of Selmar had been enough to make me absolutely determined to find a map.

At last I reached the entrance hall. Slipping across it, I hesitated, for there were several hallways leading off from it. But only one was lit by greenish candles. I hurried along it to the door at the end, then into the waiting room where Willie had left me. I listened at the door that led to Madam Vega's office before unlocking it. There was neither fire nor candles, but the room was bright with moonlight coming through the windows behind the desk. I crossed the room and felt for the latch that worked the door in the paneling alongside the fireplace. I would have liked to leave it open, but it was too much of a risk. Stepping into the musty hall, I closed it and was plunged into inky blackness. I groped my way along the short hall to the other door. This time I exerted a tiny farsensing probe to make sure the chamber beyond was empty. I could sense no one, but that did not mean the doctor or someone else was not there, sleeping. It was almost impossible to sense a sleeping presence.

I opened the door carefully and froze at the sight of firelight flickering on the walls. But then I saw that there was only a dying fire in the enormous hearth, and no lanterns or candles. I glanced around the room and my eyes fell on the portrait of Marisa Seraphim. Closing the door behind me, I crossed the room to look more closely at it.

The dim, shifty light cast by the flames made it seem as if her eyes followed me. I thought she looked less cold than before. Indeed, it seemed to me now that there was a gleam of amusement in the set of her mouth and heavily lidded yellow eyes. Reminding myself that I had not come to look at a painting, I turned to scan the room, trying to remember where I had spotted the maps. The trouble was that there were so many books and papers. So many tables and shelves. A closer look revealed that I had been right in thinking many of the books had come from the Beforetime. Such books were forbidden now, but there had been a time when the ban had not been so strict and unilateral. This collection must have been amassed in that time. Impulsively, I reached out and took one from the shelves. As I remembered from the few tattered books my mother had possessed, the pages were thin and silky smooth and the scribing impossibly small and perfect. Who could guess how long it had taken to scribe it?

The book itself turned out to be uninteresting being filled with diagrams, symbols, and words that made no sense to me. On the book's spine I read "Basic

Computer Programming" without comprehension. The next book I took up was much the same, except that the diagrams were beautifully colored.

Faintly disappointed, I moved to a different section of the shelves and took out more books at random. Many had been underlined and notated in a neat, sharp script in the margins, but none of them said anything I could understand. It seemed to me that there were as many numbers as words in them. Whatever they were about, I finally concluded, they were a far cry from the Oldtime storybooks and fictions my mother had read to Jes and me.

Suddenly I remembered where I had seen the maps. They had been on a table by the fire, where the doctor had rummaged for a pencil. My memory proved accurate, but the maps were of little use, being only badly tattered Beforetime maps. But on one I noticed that the spaces between places were covered in small faded ink notes in the same handwriting as in the Beforetime books. Maps of the Beforetime were nothing but curios, and yet someone clearly had been making an immense and determined effort to find some place that had existed in the Beforetime. A vain thing to attempt, for everyone knew the shape of the world had been changed forever by the Great White.

I wondered suddenly if these notes had been scribed by Alexi or Madam Vega. But when I looked at the scribing on the maps again, I saw that it was faded with age.

Suddenly a picture came into my mind of the pot-mender who had seemed so familiar to me, and I remembered where I had seen him before. He had been the older man with Daffyd, the boy I had met at the

Sutrium Councilcourt. It seemed too much of a coincidence that Daffyd and I had spoken of Obernewtyn, and now here was the man that had been with him. I shook my head, reminding myself that this was not the time and place for solving such puzzles. At last, I found a book of modern maps. I opened it, but to my disappointment, they were all of the lowlands. I was about to replace the book when I noticed an inscription that read, "To Marisa."

Marisa! Impulsively, I opened another book to the front page and found the same inscription. It was the same in a Beforetime book. Amazed, I understood that the collection had belonged to Marisa Seraphim. Then it struck me that the crabbed notes I had been reading were hers. I turned back to the painting, and Marisa's eyes mocked me in the light of the dying embers.

I began to search again, and this time I was startled to find that one set of shelves swung like a door. Behind it was another enormous chamber. I saw the unmistakable gleam of metal amid a pile of papers. And sure enough, it was an arrowcase. Delighted, I thrust it into my pocket. Then I noticed a square steel box standing on legs in a niche between two shelves. It was a metal cupboard with a lock built into the door. Curious, I knelt down and worked the tumblers with my mind. It was more complex than the door locks, but the mechanism was more delicate and therefore needed less force. In a moment, the door clicked open.

There were only two shelves inside, and both were stuffed with old papers and letters. I was disappointed, but I pulled out several pages. On top of the rest was a letter. It read:

My darling,

*I have bitterly thought this over, and I have
decided we cannot meet again. Mine is a strange
family, tainted with madness. I do not want you to
be part of that. I am the Master of Obernewtyn, and
I belong here, but you do not. It would destroy you
to be here. Forget what has passed between us.
My mother has arranged a marriage. The lady in
question does not love me. This is best, for, Lud
knows, I do not love her. She bonds for gold, and I
for convenience.*

The letter ended suddenly halfway down the page,
which suggested it had never been completed. I wondered why, and which Master of Obernewtyn had
penned it. Not Stephen Seraphim, certainly, and not
Lukas Seraphim. So it must be his son, Michael. And
the mother he mentioned must be Marisa.

I found two more letters among the papers. Both
had been opened and replaced neatly in their en-
velopes. One was a missive from Lukas Seraphim to his
wife, Marisa, and the other was addressed to Michael
Seraphim. I had no chance to read either, though, because I heard the sound of a muffled voice.

I quickly closed the door on the cabinet, the forgotten letters falling from my lap. There was no time to re-
open the cupboard and replace them, so I thrust them
in the narrow space beneath it and crept to the edge of
the hinged shelves. My heart pounded at the knowledge that I was trapped.

But the voices faded without anyone coming into
the doctor's chamber. Relieved, I waited until the
voices had faded completely and then made my way

back to my own room as fast as I could. Twice I had to conceal myself as older Misfits passed. By the time I was in my own bed, I was soaked with sweat and dizzy with fatigue. But even as I drifted to sleep, I seemed to see Selmar's dead eyes, gazing emptily at me.

I slept only two hours before being wakened. I had missed firstmeal, and there was no chance to talk to Matthew and Dameon, for they had already been taken through the maze to the farms. Nor had I any opportunity to speak to them at midmeal, for there were other people clustering about them. Too tired to eat, I stretched out in a patch of shade and slept, waking only when everyone was returning to their labor.

It was not until nightmeal that I finally had the chance to speak with them, but before I could whisper my news, Matthew leaned across the table and told me softly that the new Misfit was sitting at the next table. I looked where he had indicated, and my exhaustion fell away in my shock, for I knew that face.

It was Rosamunde! She seemed to sense my gaze and looked up. As I had expected, she recognized me. What I did not expect was the look of blank bitterness she gave me.

✦ 18 ✦

It was several days before I had the opportunity to speak to Rosamunde.

After that first meal, she did not come to the same sitting. I only saw her from a distance on the farms once or twice; then at last, one midmeal I saw her come out of a barn to collect her lunch. I followed and sat down beside her.

"What do you want?" she asked listlessly.

"Do you know me?" I said in a low voice.

"You are Elspeth Gordie," she said flatly.

Bewildered by her manner, I leaned closer and asked, "Is it Jes? Has something happened to him?"

"I don't want to talk to you," Rosamund said dully.

I bit my lip and suppressed an urge to shake her. "He would not have let you come here alone. He cared about you," I said. Her face trembled with some feeling, so I pressed her. "He's my brother. You must tell me if he's all right."

She looked away from me. "Leave me alone," she whispered.

"I know that you denounced me," I said, desperate to get a response from her.

Her face paled a little. "You knew?" Then the bitterness I had seen that first day in the kitchen returned to her eyes. "Of course you knew. You read my mind. I should have guessed you were like him," she said colorlessly.

I reeled at her words. "Are you saying that *Jes* can read your mind?" I said at last.

She gave a heavy sigh. "All right. I might as well tell you everything, though I wonder why you don't just read my mind and find out for yourself."

I glanced around uneasily, but no one was close enough to have heard what she was saying.

She looked up at me with sudden pathetic appeal, and for a second I saw the old Rosamunde. "You know, we were so happy in the beginning, before he found out what he was. It didn't matter about us being orphans, because soon we would get Normalcy Certificates. Then the boy came. Harald." The deadness returned to her features.

"Who was he?" I prompted.

"Just a boy, but somehow he was different from the rest of us. Nobody liked him much, because he would speak when he ought to have stayed silent, or he would refuse to do something or argue with a Herder. You could see he would never get a Certificate. Jes didn't like him any more than I did, to begin with. Then all of a sudden, they were the greatest friends. I couldn't understand it. But when I asked Jes about it, he just changed the subject. He became secretive and evasive. I did not see him as often, and there was a barrier between us when we were together.

"One day, he broke down and told me. He said, 'I have been afraid to tell you, but I love you and I must tell you the truth. I am a Misfit by birth.' I thought he was joking, and I laughed. But he wasn't. He wasn't!"

This last was almost a sob. "He said Harald had shown him what he was. He said he could talk to people inside their minds and hear what people were thinking. He kept saying you were right about having to use the powers once you knew they were there. I knew then that you must have been the same.

"He showed me." Her voice had risen and again I looked around uneasily and saw that a number of curious glances were being directed toward us. I longed to coerce Rosamunde into calmness, but I dared not use my powers so close to where the machine had caught hold of me before. Rosamunde got control of herself and went on more calmly. "He said he had not wanted a rift to grow between us but that Harald had not wanted me to be told. But he told Harald that he trusted me with his life. I was terrified he would read my mind and learn that I had denounced you to save him. I made him promise never to invade my mind.

"Jes started to talk about escaping. He said that Harald knew others like them, in Kinraide and in nearby towns, and that we could all run away and live somewhere where no one would find us. If he had said just the two of us, I would even have gone, but a group of us? There would have been a massive search. He didn't care. He said the Herders knew something about Misfits like them and that they wanted to know more. He said the boy claimed some Misfits had been taken to Herder Isle because they had given themselves away."

She fell silent for a while, and I did not prompt her. Now that she had begun, I knew she would say it all.

"Jes told me one day that a group of orphans from the home in Berrioc had been uncovered and betrayed. Those taken were friends of Harald's. They had been taken to the Herder cloister in Kinraide to be interrogated, and Jes said he and Harald were going to escape and try to help them. It was madness. A nightmare! How could two orphans break into a Herder Cloister?

"Jes said I would never understand because I was not like them. He said he and Harald had heard the others calling out for help as they were taken to the cloister." She paused with deep sadness in her eyes. "I guess I knew then what I had really known since the whole thing started. Jes loved me, but it was as if I came from another race. In some ways, Jes was hard like a stone. He told me he had rejected you because you were different. He regretted that, yet now he did the same to me because I was different in another way.

"The night they meant to go, he came to ask me to leave with them. I loved him so much that I almost said yes. But I knew it would be no good. I refused, and he climbed out the window. Harald was waiting in the garden. And that is when the soldierguards got them."

My heart froze.

"They killed Harald. Then I saw Jes shot in the chest with an arrow. He tried to run, but he was too badly hurt. One of the soldierguards ran to where he had fallen. I heard him tell Jes the Herders would be pleased to hear they had taken him alive, for they knew there were others at Kinraide and he would be made to tell their names. That was when Jes did something to the soldierguard. I don't know what. The man just stopped laughing and fell down dead. Then another soldierguard shot Jes through the throat."

Rosamunde's voice was like cold death, and I wondered numbly if that was the end of her dreadful tale. But she went on. "I wanted to die, too. They knew he had been with me, and at first they thought I was like Jes. They wanted me to tell them who the others were, but Jes had never told me. I kept telling them I didn't know. But they didn't believe me. They took me to Sutrium. They tortured me. They wanted to know all about Jes. All he could do. I told them everything, and in the end I wanted to die. I tried to make myself die. Then they sent me here."

She saw the question in my eyes and shook her head. "I didn't tell them about you. Not because I was trying to save you. It just didn't occur to me. I would have told them if they asked. But I think they will figure it out in the end, and then they will come to question you as well." Two tears slipped down her cheeks, and she did not wipe them away. "They will come for you, because they are frightened of Misfits like Jes," she said. "Because of what he could do, and because he could pass for normal."

I stood up without a word and walked stiffly into the barn. It was empty, and I threw myself into a loose bale of hay and wept. I cried for the pity of Jes's end, and for all that had been done to Rosamunde, and for Jes's friends, who must now be living in fear of discovery. I remembered my prediction on the day we had parted at Kinraide. I had been sure I would never see Jes again, but foolishly I had imagined the loss to be his, not mine.

I sensed Sharna nearby, seeking entrance to my thoughts. "Sharna," I cried bitterly to him, "why is life so full of pain and danger? There seems no end to it. Where are peace and safety in the world?"

"It would take a wiser beast than me to answer that," he told me, nuzzling my arm sweetly.

"Then teach me to be wise, for I cannot bear this pain," I sent, and looking into his sad shaggy face, I opened my mind so that he would see what I had learned.

"It is a hard thing to lose a brother," he sent, and oddly, I felt he really understood what I felt. Then he told me with compassion that wisdom was not something one could teach, but a thing each person must discover for himself.

"I can't bear that he died like that," I sent.

"Death comes in a thousand forms," Sharna sent. "All who live, not only beasts, live with death riding on their back, though none knows what face it will show for them until the moment they face it. But beasts do not fear death or regard it as a burden. Only the funaga think death is evil. But it is nature. Evil exists only in life. There is much good and evil allotted to each life, and there is much that is neither good nor bad. Death is such a thing as that." He licked me roughly, then left me alone with my grief.

"What has happened?" came Rushton's voice.

I knew that I ought to get up and make some excuse for my tears. But anger flowed through me at the thought of him reporting to Madam Vega that I had made friends, and my pain became a raging fury.

I sat up and glared at him through swollen eyes. "Nothing has happened that you need to report to your mistress," I hissed. "I am not planning to kill anyone or burn down your precious farms. There is no dire plot in hand. Nothing . . . of any importance has happened. I have just heard my brother has been murdered." My rage died as quickly as it had begun, and I lay my head down and wept anew.

After a long moment, I heard the hay rustle and opened my eyes to see Rushton kneeling in the hay beside me. He reached out and touched my arm as gently as he had ever touched a hurt animal. "I suppose you will not believe it, but I am no informant," he said. "I am sorry about the death of your brother. You must think badly of me to imagine I have no compassion, though it's true I have cared for few since the death of my mother."

I was so astonished by his gentleness and his words that my tears stopped. Rushton went on in the same soft, low voice. "My life since my mother's death has been given to anger and cold purpose. I could almost envy your affection for your brother, though now it brings you pain. . . ."

His voice faded, and for a long moment he said nothing, only staring into my eyes with his searching gaze. Then he bent closer until his breath fanned my face, his eyes probing.

"Why do you plague me?" he whispered, as if I were a dream or a wraith.

I shook my head, bewildered by the tenderness in his tone, and he sat back abruptly.

"Come now. You must return to work," he said gruffly but not unkindly. "It is not wise to grieve too long. I am no tattletale, but there are many who are."

He was as brisk as ever, but strangely his manner no longer offended me. I rose, feeling empty of all emotion. Rushton sent me to a distant field alone to check the foot of a horse he said might be going lame and bade me walk him very slowly back to the stables.

As I walked, I realized that I believed Rushton when he had said he was not an informant. Any number of

Misfits knew of my friendships and might have spoken of them to Madam Vega; Rushton had only warned me that it was dangerous making friends too openly. It was my resentment of him that had made me jump to the conclusion that he had spoken to Madam Vega.

Remembering that he was Enoch's friend, I considered asking him to inquire about Maruman. But even if my fear and hatred of Rushton were misplaced, I could not believe there was true friendship between us or any kind of easiness that would allow me to ask for his help.

Perhaps it was only because Maruman was so much on my mind, and I was still raw at the news of Jes's death, but the next morning I awoke with Maruman's dear grizzled face in my mind, his golden eyes clearly reflecting the jagged mountain range that lay between us. I told myself it was only the wisp of a dream, but what if I was wrong? What if Maruman was gazing at the mountains and longing for me as I was for him? What if he decided to try to find me?

✦ 19 ✦

THE FINAL WEEKS of harvest passed swiftly as everyone worked hard and long to complete preparations for the wintertime. The pain I had felt at learning of Jes's death had faded all too quickly; it was as if a memory had died rather than a person, because I had already accepted that I would never see him again. I had been nervous that Rosamunde would say something that would reach the ears of Madam Vega, but after that one conversation, she seemed to retreat into the silent blankness that I supposed was the reason she was sent to Obernewtyn.

I had finally, and with some trepidation, told Matthew and Dameon what Rosamunde had told me about Jes. Like me, they felt the soldierguard's death could not have happened as she had described. I could exert force enough to open a lock, and I had at last confessed my ability to coerce. But I could not possibly exert a force powerful enough to stop a person's heart or breathing. Most likely, having witnessed Jes's death and suffered torture, Rosamunde's crumbling mind had invented the vision of Jes destroying his tormentor.

No matter what had transpired that night, I feared it would eventually be discovered that Jes had a sister who had been convicted as a Misfit and sent to

Obernewtyn. I was determined to escape before that happened.

But in the meantime, the doctor or Alexi seemed to have lost interest in Cameo. She no longer disappeared, she slept more peacefully, and she grew stronger physically. A sly relationship grew between her and Matthew, and he and Dameon spoke less urgently of escape.

One midmeal, Dameon said, "It has occurred to me that if we organize our escape for the end of wintertime, just before the pass thaws, we would not have to survive the whole wintertime. I don't know how we would steal or carry enough food to sustain us for the entire season. And this way, we would only have to contend with Ariel and his wolves. With Elspeth's ability to speak with beasts and her coercion, I think we could manage to evade them."

Back and forth we talked, proposing plans, refining them, arguing, changing our minds and then changing them back again. But always Dameon was the one to make the point that ended a discussion. I had been right about him being the one to lead us.

One morning, there was a rumor at firstmeal that someone had broken into Madam Vega's chamber. I was immediately convinced that they had found the letters I had shoved under the steel cabinet in the doctor's chamber. There was no way they could trace the matter to me, but it meant I must wait a time before going back for a map. I chafed at yet another delay, but we were able to prepare for the escape in other ways. We were stealing and hiding food and supplies in a hole concealed beneath a loose board in one of the barns. We had two sacks of flour and some dried apples and potatoes, as well as two good knives and some coats and blankets.

During this period, Louis told us that things were becoming unsettled in the highlands. There were even rumors that the ghosts of the Oldtimers had been stirring restlessly on the Beforetime ruins at the edge of the Blacklands.

A ghost of a different sort, Selmar now drifted about Obernewtyn like a gray wraith, unsmiling, silent, and pale. After the initial shock of her appearance, nobody took much notice of her, and as before, she was permitted to wander freely.

Perhaps the strangest thing of all, though, was the relationship that arose between Rushton and myself. I could not like him, exactly, but his gentleness about Jes's death made me wonder why I had ever thought him a sinister figure. I had found out from Louis that he was a paid overseer who had been given the job by Madam Vega when he came to the mountains after his mother died, and sometimes I wondered at the purpose he had spoken of so fiercely.

For his part, Rushton no longer sneered at me whenever the opportunity arose. Ariel was another matter entirely. He had a queer mania that made him hurt people just to see them cringe—as though he wanted proof of his superiority. It had been even worse since he had brought Selmar back. As the days shortened, he took every opportunity to torment or hurt people, and everyone stayed out of his way as much as they could. He seemed to have forgotten about Cameo, but one day, near the end of the harvest season, he came to Cameo and bade her go with him to the doctor's chamber.

We watched her trail after him with dread.

That night, she was in her bed, but not the next night

or the one following. Soon her nightmares recommenced. I tried again to make her talk to me about what was happening to her, as did Matthew, who tortured himself with dreadful speculations. He could not bear even to look at Selmar. But Cameo refused to speak.

One night, she woke me with her mental cries, but when I went to comfort her as I had done before, I was appalled to see that her eyes were again the fierce eyes of a stranger.

"You'll never find where I hid the map." She laughed the rasping cackle of an old woman.

I stared at her. "What map?"

"Lukas said it was dangerous to think so much about the Beforetime, but I searched and I found it. I knew I would," said Cameo.

Suddenly, I realized what Cameo's altered eyes reminded me of—the yellow eyes in the portrait of Marisa Seraphim. Marisa, whose crabbed scribing was all over the Beforetime maps in the doctor's chamber.

She suddenly fell back into a natural sleep.

"It could be that she muddled our talk of needing a map with something she heard when she was in the doctor's chamber," Dameon said the next day. "If she was hypnotized, she would be very suggestible."

"You didn't see her eyes," I insisted. "They were yellow, like the eyes in the portrait. And she laughed like an old woman!"

"Are ye tryin' to say she's being haunted by the shade of a long-dead mistress of Obernewtyn?" Matthew asked bluntly.

I stared at him, knowing that this was exactly what I did think. "I know it sounds ridiculous," I admitted.

"But I've been thinking: what if the reason Alexi and Madam Vega want a Misfit with mental abilities is they think it will help them locate something that Marisa Seraphim found and hid? This map Cameo mentioned might show where it is."

"A map to what?" Matthew wondered.

I looked at him helplessly.

Cameo's decline accelerated rapidly after that; she lost weight and color until she was as fragile and ill-looking as she had been before. One day Matthew said, "Every time we talk about Cam, ye shake yer heads an' look worried. But we're nowt doing anything. I say we should get away from Obernewtyn before it is too late for her. Maybe we can still make it to th' highlands before th' pass freezes."

Dameon shook his head. "Look at the skies. It could snow any day. We cannot take the chance of being trapped in the mountains for the entire wintertime without food enough to last. The wolves will grow hungry and daring, and Lud knows what other beasts will be on the prowl. We would have to endure cold, snow, hunger, and wild animals, not to mention pursuit. The mountains themselves would be nearly frozen solid, and the snow would keep us from being able to tell where the ground was tainted. Our only chance of surviving is to escape at the end of wintertime, as we have planned."

Regardless of when we would leave, we still needed a map. I resolved to go to the doctor's chamber again the next night. Whatever measures had been taken after the supposed break-in must surely have been eased by now, and if I had to, I would use coercion. It would not take much to prevent someone seeing me and surely it was far enough from the farms and the strange machine that had caught hold of me months before to risk it. I thought about the machine and wondered, as I had done before, if it was being used by Alexi and Madam Vega to try to trap a misfit like me. It seemed very likely. As for the machine itself, how had the Beforetimers created such a thing before the Great White had begun to cause Misfits to be born? Or had Alexi done something to adapt a Beforetime machine to his purpose? Madam Vega had spoken of his ability at dealing with Beforetime machines.

I admitted to myself that beyond my desire to secure a map, I wanted to see if I could discover what Alexi and Madam Vega were seeking. I was convinced I would find the answers to all my questions in the doctor's chamber.

· 20 ·

THE NEXT DAY, there was a story circulating that someone had tried to break into Obernewtyn. One of Ariel's
wolves had been poisoned, and another shot full of arrows. It seemed incredible and insane. Whoever would
want to attack a home for Misfits? Surely there was not
enough of value to entice robbers over the badlands,
and so close to winter!

Someone told Matthew the attackers had been the
Druid's men and that one of them had been wounded
in the clash. It seemed too far-fetched to credit, and yet
I thought of Daffyd, who had spoken so knowledge-
ably of Henry Druid, then of his uncle's visit earlier in
the year, disguised as a potmender. Was it possible that
the events were connected? Given what I knew of the
Druid, I knew he might covet the Beforetime books in
the doctor's chamber. But how could he even know
they existed?

I asked Louis what he thought, but he was in one of
his reticent moods and answered all of my questions
and speculations with shrugs and grunts.

That night, I waited until the others in my chamber
slept, opened the lock, and slipped out into the halls. It
was freezing cold, and I was shivering violently before
I had gone more than a few steps. I had got as far as the

circular entrance hall before I noticed a pungent smell in the air. I was moving along the hall to Madam Vega's waiting room when I stumbled clumsily, and all at once it came to me that the strange smell in the air was the same scent that came from the sleep candles my mother had created when Jes and I were sick. I held my breath and used my abilities to coerce the fog from my mind, guessing the precaution was the result of the break-in.

At Madam Vega's door, I forced myself to stop and listen carefully, despite the fact that my ears were beginning to buzz with my need for air. I could hear nothing, and I unlocked the door hastily. It was dark in the room beyond, for the moon was covered in a thick sludge of clouds, but the air was clear. I closed the door behind me and gasped in a great breath before continuing cautiously to the doctor's chamber. There was no one there, but the fire was burning brightly. Someone had been here not long ago.

This time I ignored the books. There were simply too many of them. I decided I would concentrate my search on the tables and their drawers. I set to work methodically, going from left to right.

In the second drawer, I found more arrowcases. Several were real compasses from the Beforetime. I pocketed a very small one with a cracked case, reasoning it would not be missed and that it would not hurt to have two.

Eventually, I came to a drawer containing a pile of modern maps. I took them out and began to leaf through them. There were dozens of them, and among them I found at last a map of the mountain region. It showed all of the mountains around Obernewtyn and even a sliver of the highlands, including a bit of the White Valley. I saw that the valley where Obernewtyn stood was only one of a series of valleys going high and deep into the mountains. I had not expected the area to be so big, and I felt a surge of relief, for surely we could find a place to hide. Resisting the urge to stand there poring over the map, I folded it and pushed it down my shirt, and I returned the rest to their drawer. Then I thought of the letters I had thrust under the metal cabinet.

I crossed to the bookshelf and entered the darker room behind it. I reached into the recess under the locked cabinet and pulled out the two letters I had thrust there in a panic.

I sat back on my heels, confused. If the report about someone breaking in had not been caused by the finding of the letters, then what? Was it possible that whoever had killed Ariel's wolves had also got into Madam Vega's room? There had been no specific mention of anyone gaining access to the doctor's chamber, after all, so perhaps my carelessness wasn't to blame.

Looking down at the letters, I decided on impulse to read them. The letter to Marisa from her husband was brief, a perfunctory inquiry after her health, then a list of books he had been able to obtain for her. At the end was a veiled suggestion that some of the books she wanted were dangerous, for the Herder Faction was becoming more stringent in its judgment against Beforetime artifacts.

The letter to Michael Seraphim was one page of what must have been a longer letter, and I gaped as I read it.

My friend,

I wish you would reconsider your notion to adopt young Alexi. Marisa finds him sly, and I fear I must for once agree with her. She is not motherly, of course, as you have oft said. She is too brilliant, too preoccupied with her books and researches, and seems to have little regard for her grandson, but she is still your mother. I think she knows that you never loved Manda and regrets your unhappiness. Now that Manda is dead, can you not bond again? Stephen is very young and would accept a stepmother, I am sure. What of the village girl you loved? Can you not seek her out?

Slowly I pushed the letter back into its envelope and replaced them both in the cabinet, astounded that Alexi was the adopted son of Michael Seraphim, the second Master of Obernewtyn. No wonder Alexi had spoken with such arrogance. He was more than the doctor's "assistant"—they were legal brothers. How it must gall him to know that, by lore, only blood relatives could inherit property.

A slight scraping sound interrupted the thought, and I froze. The noise came again, and I crept across to the dividing shelf and peered into the main chamber. The door was closed fast, but to my utter amazement the entire huge fireplace suddenly swung open to reveal a descending staircase. I backed away and climbed under a table in a dark corner, my heart hammering. Hunched down as I was, I discovered that I could see the movement of legs and feet in the adjoining chamber. I could not tell if they were men or women, but there were four of them, and I saw the glitter of melting snow as they removed their coats. The passage they had used must lead outside.

The fireplace swung back into place, and when they spoke, I recognized their voices.

"I could have sworn I heard something as we came in," said Ariel.

"Don't be a fool," came Alexi's deep voice. "How could anyone come here without succumbing to the sleep candles?"

"Thank Lud we banked up the fire. It gets colder every time we go out, and now we have the snow to contend with," said Madam Vega irritably.

The fourth person said nothing, but I could see she was a women. Was it Guardian Myrna?

"What are you going to do about the Druid's man?" Ariel asked.

"You can put his body out for the wild wolves," said Madam Vega. "I do not know what the old man hoped to achieve in sending him up here."

Alexi laughed. "I expect he fears that we are closer to the knowledge he seeks than he likes."

"We don't know for sure if the Druid is even alive. It could simply be his followers," Vega said.

"That's not what his man said," Ariel laughed unpleasantly.

"Either way, I don't like the competition. It's a pity we can't call the Council in to clear them up," said Madam Vega.

"Impossible," Alexi said coldly. "Soldierguards up here would make our search impossible. And imagine if they found out what we planned. It is hard enough to keep those nosy Herders from Darthnor out."

"Well, tonight was a waste of time as far as the search goes," Ariel said. "I told you she would be useless."

"I did not think to achieve anything. I merely wanted to try out the new configuration of the machine, and I don't want to ruin Cameo as we have this one," he added. I understood then that the silent fourth must be poor Selmar.

"I'm sick of her and all of these Misfits," Ariel said petulantly. "I am tired of guiding them through the maze and back and of listening to their idiocies."

"They keep Stephen happy, thinking he has some humanitarian cause," said Madam Vega. "And when the time comes, they will be good labor. Marisa thought the things we seek would be buried, and I have no intention of digging them up like a common farmer. Besides, it would have been impossible to suddenly stop purchasing Misfits without the Council wondering what was going on. And you must admit, the business of searching the orphan homes makes the perfect cover for our search for the right Misfit." She paused thoughtfully. "You really think it was Cameo who set off the Zebkrahn that day?"

"It would have taken a high level of mental power to engage the machine and then to escape it, and I would not have thought her capable of it," said Alexi. "But she has been dreaming about machines since it happened, according to our informant. It must be that she's hiding the true extent of her abilities. But once we use the Zebkrahn on her directly, the pretense will end."

"I'll be relieved when our search is done," Vega said.

"Damn that Marisa. If it wasn't for her, we would have had the map long ago," Alexi said angrily.

Madam Vega laughed. "Can you really blame her? It was she who discovered the location of the Beforetime weaponmachines, after all. A pity she was content to map their location and nothing more. Hiding the map from us was her sour idea of a joke . . . and I suspect she thought the knowledge would keep her alive," she said.

"She misjudged my patience," snarled Alexi. "I only hope she didn't destroy the map."

"She would never destroy knowledge," Vega said with confidence.

They stood with their backs to my hiding place, warming their hands and silent for the moment. I thought about what I had overheard. Alexi, Madam Vega, and Ariel were seeking Beforetime weapon-machines, and so too, it seemed, was Henry Druid. But why?

I thought of the machine they had spoken about— the Zebkrahn. This must be the machine that had caught hold of my mind. I shuddered at the thought of such a thing being used on Cameo. And yet maybe it would not harm her, since she did not have the power they sought.

Suddenly, I realized that Selmar had left the fire and was drifting toward the dividing shelves. To my horror, she knelt down and peered through the gap to where I was hiding. I doubted she could see me, but somehow she knew I was there. I held my breath.

"I'm so tired I can hardly keep my eyes open," Madam Vega said with a yawn.

"Get her away from the books," snapped Alexi.

Ariel came over and pulled Selmar to her feet. She went, unresisting as he led her away. To my relief, they all left the doctor's chamber, but I was so unnerved by what had happened that it was almost morning before I could summon the courage to come out of my hiding place and creep back to my room.

I hid the map behind a loose stone in the wall near my bed, and then I lay down and watched the sky lighten through the slot window.

In the end, I fell asleep, and woke a short time later wishing I had not. I felt heavy-eyed and sluggish, and I had to splash my face with freezing water to rouse my wits. Cameo tried to tell me of a dream she'd had, but I forestalled her, saying she could tell me later.

If I had known what was to come, I would have listened.

· 21 ·

I ATE ALONE at firstmeal, having missed the first sitting, and was put to work at once by Rushton when I arrived on the farms. But when midmeal came, I hastened to sit with Matthew and Dameon, wanting to tell them what I had discovered. Before I could speak, however, Dameon asked coolly whether I had been out the previous night.

"Yes, but how did you know?" I asked, puzzled.

"You were careless," he said.

"No!" I said indignantly.

"You promised me that you would take care," Dameon said. "And now the decision has been made to release Ariel's wolf-dogs every night."

"Wait," I said. "Last night I went to the doctor's chamber. I heard Alexi and Madam Vega talking, but I'm sure they didn't see me. They had captured a man Henry Druid had sent here; he's after the same thing they are. *That* must be why they decided to put the dogs out."

"Henry Druid?" Matthew echoed, at the same time as Dameon asked what they were all searching for.

"Beforetime weaponmachines," I said. "I don't know why, but right now our biggest problem is that Alexi and Madam Vega are the ones who control the machine that caught hold of my mind that time. Tomorrow night, they are going to use it on Cameo, thinking it will force her to reveal hidden Misfit powers. Somehow, they imagine Cameo can help them find the weaponmachines—or at least Marisa Seraphim's map that shows where they are."

"But Cameo knows nowt of any map," Matthew said. He glanced over to where she sat farther along the bench, plaiting grass in her thin fingers, her eyes on the hazy line of mountains visible beyond the stark branches of the trees in the nearest orchard.

Dameon coughed, and we both looked at him. "I have been thinking about what is being done to Cameo. What if they think they can use Misfit powers to raise the ghost of Marisa Seraphim?"

"But . . . that is not possible," I said.

"No, but they do not know that."

"Wait!" Matthew said, eyes glittering with excitement. "What if it's nowt the ghost of her that they are seeking, but simply traces of her mind? Dameon, ye told me once that ye can pick up echoes of feelings from objects."

Dameon nodded, but said that feelings could not give them any useful information.

I nodded slowly, too. "If they are strong, thoughts leave an echo as well." I wondered if Matthew had hit upon the right answer. Certainly, Marisa's books and papers would be full of her thoughts and impressions, and I knew that if I desired it, I could probably read those thoughts. But how could Alexi and Madam Vega know so much about Misfit powers? Was it possible that Madam Vega divined it because of her own unacknowledged Misfit ability?

"We mun leave tonight," Matthew said urgently. "Perhaps if Henry Druid has a secret camp in the mountains, we can join him. Or at least raid his supplies."

"Perhaps we have no choice," Dameon said. "I just wish we had managed to get a map."

Triumphantly, I told them about the map I had found. That decided Dameon, who said the supplies we had collected would have to do. We would bring whatever of our stored supplies we could conceal and carry back through the maze that evening. I would come and unlock their doors that night and do any coercing needed, and we would then make our way to the front of the house and go out the same way we had come in—through the front gate. Despite everything, the audacity of the plan pleased me.

That afternoon, as we gathered to be taken back through the maze to the house, snow began to fall lightly and softly, whitening the world. Uneasily, I looked out to the mountains, my breath making little puffs of mist in the cold air. Their tips were white, too, barely visible against the pale sky.

"In case you have any notion of escape," Ariel said, so close that the hair on my neck stood on end, "I should warn you again about the mountains and the wild wolves. I have seen them tear rabbit and deer apart while literally on the run. No one has ever been mad enough to try to escape in this season." He ran his fingers through his white-blond hair, a languid movement that lent his cruelty a casual air.

I looked away from him, certain he must have been able to hear my heart hammering in my chest. Behind us, the imprints made by our boots were already filling up with a fresh drift of velvety white snow. I told myself that whatever Ariel guessed from my expression as I had looked out at the mountains, he could not possibly know we were plotting an escape that very night.

But we did not go that night, for at midmeal, Sly Willie came for Cameo, and there was nothing any of us could do but watch as she was led away. Matthew looked so openly distraught that I kicked him under the table. There was no chance to talk until we got to the farms the next morning, and I was shocked to see they were covered in a thick white blanket of snow. We seemed to have gone in a matter of days from summerdays to wintertime.

"We mun help her," Matthew said, seeming not to see the transformation.

"Tonight I will see if I can find out where she is," I promised, just as Rushton arrived to send us off on our various errands. He seemed distracted, and it occurred to me that he had been that way for some time, but I was too worried about Cameo to ponder it deeply. I found myself among a group sent to round up the small herd of goats, which were to be led through the maze to a small yard adjacent to the house. I was in one of the farthest fields, having just found a lame goat, when it began to snow hard. It took me a long time to get her back to the stable, and when I'd done so, I was shivering with the cold.

Rushton heard me cough, took one look at me, and sent me up to the house with an older Misfit to see Guardian Myrna. By night, I was running a high fever, my voice was a painful croak, and I had been put into a sick chamber. There was no question of going out to look for Cameo, and I finally fell into a fitful sleep in which red birds swooped at my face and the ground opened up malevolently and tried to swallow me.

The first person I saw when I woke was Rushton. "You are awake at last," he said. "The horses missed you."

I frowned, wondering how long I had slept. Then I wondered why he was visiting me.

Before I could ask, Guardian Myrna came in. Rushton sat up slightly and said in a clipped voice, "Try to remember exactly what medicines you gave that lame horse." She went out again, and Rushton leaned close. "I told her I wanted to talk to you about a farm matter, but that isn't true. I came to give you this."

He held out a small cloth bag. I took it and opened it, and a wonderful summery smell filled the air. He closed my hands around the package and urged me to keep it hidden and eat it when no one was around. "It will help you regain strength quickly," he said, and then without another word, he left.

Later I drew the bag open and looked inside to find a moistened ball of herbs. My mother had made such things, and I pondered the fact that Rushton would give me medicine that was so obviously the product of forbidden herb lore. I come to the conclusion that he genuinely wanted to help me. Certainly the ball of herbs would do me no harm, and indeed that night, I slept deeply and well.

When I woke, it was night again and my head was clear. Guardian Myrna came in and, seeing I was awake, examined me and said brusquely that I might as well go back to my own chamber and sleep, for she needed the beds.

I arrived in my room as the others were changing for

the nightmeal. There was a queer solemnity in their faces, and I asked with some trepidation if something had happened. I was afraid for Cameo, of course, for there was no sign of her. But one of the girls came close and whispered, "Selmar is dead. She tried to run again, but Ariel got her. He . . . shot her so she couldn't run, then . . . set his wolves loose."

"He couldn't . . . ," I whispered, sickened.

"Some of us saw it," said the other girl. Her face was ashen as she spoke, and I thought mine must look the same. I was still sitting on the side of my bed, alone and too shattered by what I had been told to eat, when Matthew came in. His face was haggard. I got to my feet at once, alarmed, and asked him if it was true that Ariel had let his wolves kill Selmar. He bowed his head. "He . . . he keeps boastin' about it like it was a good joke on her." Then he faltered and seemed to find it hard to speak.

I knew he must be worrying himself ill over Cameo, and I laid my hand on his shoulder. "I will go out and look for her tonight. I promise."

He shook his head, and when he looked at me, his eyes were full of compassion. A thrill of fear shot thought me.

"The Council have found out about ye, Elspeth," he said, answering the question he saw in my face. "That is what I came to tell you. I overheard Sly Willie tellin' Lila in the kitchen just now. Some soldierguards arrived about an hour ago an' they have been with Madam Vega ever since. She sent Willie fer a meal for them." He went on to say that two Councilmen were due to arrive the following morning, and I was to be ready for them to take away at once. "It seems they want to make sure they have ye down from th' mountains before the pass is completely closed. I came to tell ye that ye mun escape tonight, Elspeth," Matthew said. "Willie thinks yer still in the sick chamber, an' he told Lila that Madam Vega insists ye mun stay there fer the night. I've a bag of supplies an' a blanket and a tinder box stashed in the bottom of the linen cupboard for ye. It's not enough, but hopefully we will nowt be long after ye."

"But what about the rest of you? Cameo . . ." I stopped, seeing anguish flood his eyes. "Cameo?"

He shook his head and his expression grew bleak. "Ye ken as well as I do what they meant to do to her. Days have passed since Ariel took her away, an' no one has seen a hair of her since. I mun face . . . we mun face the fact that they have used th' machine on her."

"You can't just give up on her," I said.

"I will not. I dinna! But I am sayin' that there is nothing you can do now, Elspeth. Ye mun save yerself."

"At . . . at dusk each day, I will farseek you," I stammered, hardly able to believe that all our careful plans had come to this. I gathered my wits and got the map from behind the stone. Matthew tried to refuse it, but I insisted, telling him I had already looked at the map and I had a second compass. "This mountain valley runs up into another, and that runs into another beyond that. The valleys go much farther into the mountains than you would guess. I will go high and deep and try to find a cave."

Matthew nodded and pushed the map into his shirt, his eyes dark with apprehension. "Be careful."

"You too," I said. "Say goodbye to the others for me."

"Ye ken I will," he said. We stared at each other helplessly for a moment, and then he suddenly threw his arms around me and hugged me hard. "I love ye like a sister, Elspeth," he said gruffly into my ear, his accent very strong. Then he released me and strode away.

Deciding I had better not linger where I was, I slipped out into the hall and went to wait in an empty chamber I had noticed as I came from the healing room. The door stood open, and I sat on the floor behind it. I could feel nothing, not even grief for poor Cameo. I listened to the sound of people returning from their meal and then readying themselves for bed. I stayed still and quiet when one of the senior Misfits extinguished most of the hall candles and locked the doors. They did not trouble with the empty room. I waited until I could hear neither voice nor footfall, and then I stood up and got the supplies Matthew had left for me. I headed for the front entrance hall and the main doors, determined to coerce anyone who got in my way.

But all at once I heard the voices of Madam Vega and of Ariel. My heart gave a leap of fear, and I turned swiftly and ran down a short hall. Opening the first door I came to, I was startled to find a set of steps winding up. I ran to the second level and then to the third, slowing down when I saw light at the top, but it was only a lantern hung on the wall of a corridor. I decided to go along the passage and see if I could find other steps leading down, closer to the front door.

I had not gone far when, very quietly, a voice spoke behind me.

"If you make one sound, I will kill you." To my utter terror, I felt the tip of something sharp press into my neck.

PART III

✦

THE MASTER OF OBERNEWTYN

◆ 22 ◆

"Nod if you will not cry out," the voice said.

With a queer sense of desolation, I recognized whom that whispered voice belonged to. I moved my mouth to speak, but the hand over my mouth tightened. Limply, I nodded.

He unlocked a door beside us and propelled me into a small but lavish bedchamber. Candles were lit and a fire warmed the air.

I stared about me with a kind of despair, for this was not the room of any hired servant. Like the rest of Obernewtyn, the room was hewn of gray stone, but unlike those in the chambers of Misfits, the window in this room was wide and would afford a view, too, though now the shutters were pulled across to keep out the cold night air. The floor was covered in a thick, beautiful rug, and the table and chairs and the comfortable couch were enough to make anyone suspicious.

Forgetting my initial fear, I turned angrily to stare at my captor—Rushton.

"I thought you worked for pay," I said accusingly.

He shrugged, seemingly unashamed of himself. "My position here is . . . ambiguous," he said softly. "Keep your voice down," he added.

Outrage gave way to confusion. If he didn't want us

to be heard, then he must not intend to denounce me. I watched him warily as he crossed to the front of the fire. He poked at the embers with a stick, and gradually I went closer.

He looked up at me, the firelight flickering over his grim face. "You don't seem frightened. Are you?" he asked.

"No," I said simply, because it was true. I felt too numb. He gestured for me to sit on the couch, and I shook my head. Uttering a growl, he moved swiftly, plonking me unceremoniously onto the seat.

"Then you are a fool," he said. I looked up at him resentfully. "Only a fool would not be afraid in your situation. I could have been one of the guardians. . . ."

My anger and bewilderment melted at his grave tone.

He sat down opposite me. "It is time for us to talk. Lud knows we should have done so before now." He shook his head as if at his own folly.

"Why were you sneaking around in the dark?" he asked with some of his old haughtiness. I bridled at his tone and gave him a sullen look that made him frown.

"I ought to march you off to Madam Vega right now," he said, but his tone was one of weary contempt, empty of threat. "You have caused me a great deal of trouble, and it might be the best thing to let them have you. I knew there would be trouble the first time I saw you," Rushton added. "And Louis warned me. . . ."

I stared. "Louis warned you about me?"

He actually smiled at that. "It is rather late in the day to become cautious, Elspeth. He said you were curious as a cat, and so you are. Perhaps I should tell you that I know Alexi is searching for a Misfit with particular abilities to help him find something hidden. I believe you have the abilities he seeks, and I suspect he finally knows that."

I gaped, my heart thundering. How could he know so much? "I . . . I don't know what you mean," I faltered.

He lifted his dark brows skeptically. "I am also aware that the Council has sent men to bring you to Sutrium. And I can guess that your friends have been unable to help you except to advise you to run, as far and as fast as you can. It is wise advice, for it appears the Council is very interested in Misfits like you—there are far more of you than most realize. The Council interrogates them, then burns them, or they are given to the Herders who carry them off to Herder Isle."

I looked at him dumbly, aware that I was shivering from fear. Seeing that I made no effort to deny what he said, he nodded slightly and continued.

"Your only option is to get away tonight, but I tell you quite simply that you have no hope unless you put yourself in my hands and do as I say."

"Who are you? Why would you help me?" I asked.

He gave me a guarded look. "It is enough for you to know that I am no enemy to you. Or to your suspicious friends, though you have jeopardized my own plans with your endless questions and curiosity. Rest assured I do not share the ambitions of Vega and Alexi to dig up the past. It is better dead and buried."

"Plans?" I asked, and unexpectedly he smiled.

"Even now you are curious," he said, his tone half amused and half exasperated. "I wonder if you really understand how much danger you face. Louis was right. You are curious to the point of foolishness." All at once, a sad sort of tenderness softened his eyes. "Selmar was curious, too, when she first came. Always asking questions and poking her nose into everything. She near drove Louis mad in the beginning. So hungry for answers, whatever the cost—and it proved dear."

"I can't help what life has made of me," I said defensively.

He stood abruptly. "Come. There is no more time for talk."

"What am I to do, then?" I asked.

Rushton handed me a thick gray cloak from a wall peg. "You'll need a heavier coat. It is impossible for you to leave the grounds tonight. The weather will get worse before it gets better and even an arrowcase would not help you, for the storms that run from the Blacklands affect the bearings. Nor can you go through the pass if you managed to find your way there, for it is white with snow, and though not yet completely blocked, it will be impossible to see where the ground is too badly tainted to cross on foot." He spoke calmly and deliberately. "I cannot let you stay here, either, because the house will be searched from top to bottom, and I am not exempt."

"Then there is nowhere for me to go," I said despairingly.

"You must remain on the farms until the weather clears. They will not be able to search there until the storm ends, and since the maze is snowed in, they are unlikely even to think of the farms to begin with. As soon as the moment is right, I will return for you, and I will tell you of a place where there are supplies enough to last you until the wintertime ends."

"But if the maze is impassable, how are we going to get to the farms?"

Rushton crossed restlessly to the window and peered through the shutter. "We will go outside the grounds and around. They won't imagine you would escape only to come back inside the walls." He frowned. "I thought I heard something. . . ." He shook his head and came back to the fire, pulling on his own coat.

"The wolves?" I asked, thinking of poor Selmar.

Rushton only smiled. "They are locked up." He looked at me searchingly. "You are pale. I hope you are properly recovered. You took the medicine I gave you?"

I nodded. "It was herb lore, wasn't it?"

"Yes," he said simply. "One of my friends has great skill in the art of healing, as did my mother. I know there is no evil in those old ways. The Council and Herder Faction are fools, frightened of everything. Now they have decided you are a danger because they don't understand you." He shook his head again and glanced out the window. "We must go now."

"Yes, I . . . ," I began, but Rushton waved his hand urgently. We both listened, and this time I heard something, too—the sound of running footsteps.

"Lud take it! I think they have discovered that you are missing. That was surely a coach I heard some while back. The Councilmen must have changed their minds about waiting in Guanette until morning. We have to get you out of the house *now,* or you will be trapped."

There was a loud knock on the door, and we both froze in horror. Rushton tore his coat off and gestured me toward the shuttered window, behind which lay a balcony. It was snowing hard outside. I pulled the door nearly shut and pressed my ear up against it.

"All right, all right," Ruston called grumpily after a second knock. "What is it?"

"Still dressed?" I heard Ariel ask him suspiciously.

"I was reading in front of the fire. I fell asleep," Rushton said casually. "What's going on? I heard a commotion."

"One of the Misfits has escaped," Ariel said. "Elspeth Gordie. Skinny girl with dark hair and a proud look. Sly bitch." There was a pause, and when Ariel spoke again, his voice was full of mistrust. "In fact, you must know her. She has been working on the farms."

My heart thumped wildly.

"I know the one you mean," Rushton said with a smothered yawn. "Quick with the horses but insolent. Anyway, why all the fuss over one Misfit? Lots more where she came from," he said coolly.

"The Council has sent some men here after her. She's wanted for questioning," Ariel said evasively.

"She'll be dead before morning if she's out in it. Storm's nearly on top of us."

"I don't doubt she will die," Ariel said viciously. "I have let the wolves out."

"A bit drastic, don't you think?" Rushton drawled through another yawn. "I suppose you want me to help look for her."

"You are paid to work," Ariel snarled.

There was a long pause. "I am paid to manage the farms," Rushton said at last, his voice cool. "But I might as well come. Otherwise I'll be up all night listening to your beasts."

"Good. It's snowing, so you'd better put on boots and a coat. I'll come back for you," he added imperiously. There was the sound of footsteps and the outer door closing; then I heard Rushton's voice.

"You can come in. He's gone."

I obeyed, shivering with cold. "He sounded suspicious," I said worriedly, but Rushton shook his head.

"He's always like that. But Alexi must want you badly to conduct a search while the Councilmen are here. Though I doubt very much that he has any intention of handing you over." Howling sounded in the distance, and he scowled. "We can't go out the front gate now, but there is one other way to get to the farms: pipes running under the maze. It is a foul labyrinth and hard going, but you are small enough to fit. The problem is there will be dogs in the courtyard, barring the way."

"Dogs or wolves?" I asked, my heartbeat quickening with hope.

"Half breeds and a few pure wolves Ariel has cowed enough that they will obey him," Rushton said in open disgust. "Why?"

"I . . . I can control them," I offered hesitantly. "With my mind."

Rushton nodded slowly, and instead of the astonishment I had expected, there was a touch of humor in his eyes. "You can control these beasts? You know they have been tormented near to madness and only obey Ariel out of terror and hunger?"

"I can manage them," I insisted with more certainty than I felt, knowing there was no other choice but to try, and the longer I stayed, the more dangerous it was for Rushton. Yet I hesitated.

"Before . . . when you caught me, you said you would kill me if I didn't cooperate," I said in a low voice. "Did you mean it?"

Rushton looked at me with the same unreadable expression I had seen on his face that day in the barn.

"It would have been safer for me if I could have," he said at last. "Best for my friends and for yours. If you are caught, you will reveal my role in your escape, for no one resists Alexi. And if the Council gets you, the Herders will make you talk. Alive you are a danger to all I have planned."

"Is your plan so important, then?" I asked softly.

"More than you could possibly imagine," Rushton answered simply.

I stared at his troubled face and willed myself to be strong. "Tell me the way through to the farms. I will not betray you. And I will manage the wolves." *Or die trying*, I thought.

"The drains run from the courtyard to the farms and are like a maze themselves, but they were not designed to confuse. Remember to always take the right turn and you will be safe. To get from here to the courtyard, you will have to use the tunnels. I am not so certain about them. My mother told me of them, but she had never seen them herself, and I have had little opportunity to explore." He explained about the tunnels, then looked up warily as footsteps echoed past his door.

"When you get to the farms, keep to the walls. The storm will be much worse by then, and if you get lost, you will die. Follow the walls to the farthest silo. The door will be open. Hide there until I come."

"But . . . but is that all? For that I am to risk wild beasts and capture?" I asked.

"You risk no more than I," Rushton said coldly.

"But what if you don't come? Where is the refuge you mentioned?" I faltered.

He shook his head regretfully. "Understand this. I have already told you too much. If I tell you any more and you are caught, I will endanger others. It is my decision to risk my life for you. I will not decide that for them."

Chastened, I nodded, for what he said was surely the truth.

"You do not know what an irony it would be if you betrayed me," Rushton said cryptically, moving to the door. He pressed his ear against the dark wood and listened before opening the door and looking out. He motioned for me to go into the hall. "Go quickly. Ariel will be coming from the other direction. I will try to direct the search toward the front of the house." Rushton looked into my eyes, and I marveled at how green his were. Like deep forest pools.

"Perhaps someday we will have the chance to talk properly," he said. "There are many things I would like—"

He stopped abruptly. We could hear footsteps again. "Go quickly," he said urgently.

"Goodbye," I whispered as I slipped away from him and descended into the darkness.

· 23 ·

I FELT MY way along the hidden passage, walking as carefully as possible, but there were several unpleasant crunches under foot that made me wonder what I was treading on. The smell and the veils of dusty cobwebs I pushed through told me that the tunnel had not been used for a very long time, and I wondered again how Rushton had known about it. The darkness was total, and I only hoped there was not a fork or turning I had missed.

Then I heard voices coming from the other side of a wall. I stopped and listened.

"She must be found," said a voice. "If it weren't for the Council . . ." It was Madam Vega.

"I am glad they came," said Alexi. "They have shown me that she is the one we have been seeking."

Ariel spoke. "She won't get past my hounds."

"I want her found, not torn to pieces. That affair with the other girl was quite unnecessary. You are a barbarian," Alexi added, almost as if he found that amusing.

"She will be found alive," Madam Vega promised soothingly.

It terrified me to hear her certainty. It did not enter any of their heads that I might get away.

"The beasts have been trained to mutilate," said Ariel sulkily. "They kill only on command."

"She must not be allowed to die," said Alexi in a flat voice that sent ice into my blood. "It might be years till another like her is found. A pity we wasted so much time on that last defective. I was so certain, but she had only minor abilities after all."

They passed out of my hearing, and despairingly, I knew they meant Cameo. What had they done to her?

I forced myself to continue. The tunnel seemed endless, but after some time I bumped headlong into a stone wall. I gave an involuntary cry as I staggered back, and then stopped to listen anxiously, fearful that someone might have heard.

"Greetings," came a thought.

My body sagged with relief and astonishment. "Sharna?" I asked incredulously.

"I dreamed you were in danger, so I came," he sent. "If you make yourself low, you can come through the wall."

I did as he suggested and felt a low gap in the wall. I reached my hand through it and brushed the soft scratchiness of a tapestry. I had never noticed it before, but when I crawled past it, I saw that I had come out in the kitchen pantry.

Sharna pressed his nose against my leg as I emerged, and I remembered what he had said.

"What did you dream about me?" I asked.

"I dreamed your life has a purpose that must be fulfilled, for the sake of all beasts," he answered.

It was late at night, and I squinted into the darkness of the kitchen, trying to see his face and thinking of the dreams Maruman had experienced in which I had

201

figured. The old cat had always insisted that my life was important to the beastworld and that it was his task to aid me and keep me safe. But I had taken this as something he had imagined in his disturbed periods.

Sharna interrupted my reflections to ask how he could help. I explained that I had to get out of the kitchen and into the courtyard adjacent to the maze. From there, I could reach the farms.

"There are beasts in the yard," Sharna returned, projecting an image of huge doglike shapes moving about, sniffing at the wall and the maze gate.

"I know. I will talk to them and ask them to let me pass," I said.

"They will not hear you," Sharna warned. "They were once wild wolf cubs, but they were caught by the funaga-li and made mad with rage. There is a red screaming in their heads that stops them from being able to hear anything but their own fury. Best to come back when they are locked up."

"I have to pass them *now*," I sent. "Maybe I can find a way to distract them long enough for me to get into the drain."

There was a long pause while he ruminated. "I will go to them," he told me at last. "Innle must be shielded." I started, because "Innle" was what Maruman sometimes called me when he spoke of my appearances in his dreams. It meant "one who seeks" in beast thought-symbols, and I had always thought it some queer term of affection.

"Come," Sharna commanded, crossing the kitchen. I followed down a short corridor and unlocked the outer door, opening it only a crack. The chill of wintertime bit deep into my skin. Then I saw the glimmer of red eyes and heard a low, savage growling that filled me with icy fear.

"Greetings, sudarta," Sharna sent, flattering them with a title that applauded their strength. It seemed to have no effect on them.

Sharna turned to me, his own eyes gleaming. "Do not go until I tell you. While you wait, find with your eyes the place you must go." Without waiting for an answer, he turned back to the door, nosed it open, and began to make an odd, low thrumming sound that vibrated in his throat. Beyond the door, I saw the red eyes withdraw.

"Sharna, what . . . ?" I began, but suddenly the old dog launched himself from the door and raced across the yard toward the wolves. Only then did I understand that he had not meant to persuade them to let me pass.

"Sharna!" I screamed. "Don't—"

"Go!" he commanded. The primitive snarling of the wolves sent a primeval shudder through my body. I heard Sharna taunting them, calling them away from my exit.

Trembling so hard I could scarcely walk, I stepped into the courtyard and stood for a moment, paralyzed with fear at the sight of the wolves falling on Sharna.

"Go!" he shouted again into my thoughts. A madness of terror roared through me as one set of red eyes turned to me and the beast uttered a growl. I flew across the courtyard, tore away the drain cover, and flung myself into the round opening behind it. Terrified one of the wolves would follow, I wriggled mindlessly along the pipe, imagining snapping jaws closing on my foot and dragging me backward.

I heard a howl of pain and stopped my mad flight. I was horrified to realize that I had left Sharna to his savage brethren.

"Go!" Sharna cried yet again, and I felt him weakening. I knew then that even if I could turn and go back, I could not help him. He had sacrificed himself for me, and I had not realized it until too late. Sick with shame and despair, I continued, but more slowly, for aside from the narrowness of the tunnel and the darkness, I was half suffocated by my tears.

In the end, I had to stop and gather myself before I could go on. The crawl through the network of pipes was such a long, cold, exhausting journey that, by the time I reached its end, sorrow and guilt over Sharna had given way to sheer dogged determination to make use of the chance he had paid for with his life.

My trousers had shredded at the knees and my palms were so raw and painful that I did not even realize I had reached the end until I tumbled out into the soft, cold snow. Gasping, I lay in the drift for a long moment, panting and weeping, but it was too cold to stay there long. My tears were already freezing on my cheeks. I managed to stand and look about, but it was impossible to tell whether it was still night, for there was nothing to see but the blinding white of the flying snow, which was a kind of darkness, too. Squinting, I tried to make out the shape of the silo, but I could not see more than two steps in front of me, and I dared not move away from the wall.

In the end, I had no choice but to climb painfully back into the hated drain, wrap myself in the coat Rushton had given me, and wait until I could see the silo. It was only slightly warmer inside, and because I lay there motionless, the icy cold soon crept into my bones. I thought of the fever I had only just thrown off, and prayed it would not return.

After a long time, the snow seemed to lessen. I still could not see the silo, but made out a shape that seemed to be the back of the milking barn. Far better to be inside it than in the drain, I decided, and I slid out into the snow. My limbs felt stiff and unwieldy, and when I tried to step forward, my legs were so slow to obey me that I fell headlong into the snow. Cursing and weeping with frustration, I gritted my teeth and forced myself to rise again. Then I began to hobble carefully toward the barn. The snow slowed, and for a moment, eerily, the moon reflected on it. Or perhaps it was a veiled sun. I saw then that it was not the milking barn ahead, but another, smaller shed I did not recognize.

It began to snow hard again. I did not change direction, because I knew that I could not be outside for much longer without falling into a deadly lethargy that would have me lie down and die, imagining I was in a warm feather bed. Reaching the shed, I found that snow had blown against it in great drifts. I had stumbled all around it before I realized with despair that the door must be buried in snow.

"Who is there?" called a voice. I staggered in a circle, trying to see who had called out.

"Is someone there?" the voice called again, marginally closer.

"I am here," I called, all at once terrified of being left alone. I saw a flash of light and broke into a shuffling run toward it.

"Who is it?" asked the voice, much closer now. Suddenly a face appeared in front of me out of the swirling whiteness. I knew him. It was an unsmiling Misfit my age named Domick. I had sometimes seen him with Rushton, I remembered, and the thought reassured me.

"Elspeth Gordie?" He held the lantern up to my face. "What are you doing here?"

I stood in the midst of the storm, my mind reeling. What could I say? What possible reason could I have for wandering around on the farms? The silence between us lengthened, and I saw suspicion form on Domick's face.

At last he said, "Well, you had better come back with me. We'll talk where it's warmer."

He struck off to the right, and I followed him closely until we reached a squat, sturdy building I had not seen before.

"What is this place?" I asked through chattering teeth.

Domick bundled me through the door. "The watch-hut," he said shortly, and hustled me across to the fire. He hauled off my snow-crusted coat and threw a thick blanket around my shoulders, then he piled more wood on the fire.

"Are you numb anywhere?" he asked. Wordlessly, I pointed to my feet. He wrestled off my boots, grimacing at the bloody mess of my knees. Both feet were white and bloodless.

"Frostbite," muttered Domick, and he began to rub them vigorously. In a short while, sensation returned with burning, painful clarity. Only when I was writhing with pain did he stop.

"You were lucky. Don't you know anything about frostbite? You could have lost a foot if you'd left them that way," he scolded.

I shuddered.

He gave me a bowl of warm water to bathe my knees and palms, and when I had finished, he pressed a mug full of soup into my hand. Then he fixed me with a disconcerting stare. "Well, what are you doing out here?" he asked.

I sipped at the soup, then looked up at him. "I've run away," I said, for there was no other answer.

He nodded. "How did you get past the maze?"

I sipped again at the drink, trying to think what to say. Though I had seen them together, I couldn't risk giving away Rushton's part in my escape.

"I . . . found some drainpipes that go under the maze," I said at last, lamely.

Suspicion hardened in his face. "I will have to report you," he said coldly. "But there is the storm. I'll lock you in until someone comes from the house."

He put me into a small room and locked the door behind him. I decided I would stay until the storm abated and Domick slept, then I would open the lock and find my way to the silo. In the meantime, there was a sacking bed in one corner. I climbed onto it gratefully, and not even my fear and despair at all that had happened could keep me awake.

· 24 ·

I SLEPT MORE deeply than I'd intended, but it was a healing sleep. When I woke, I felt rested and alert, and I lay still, enjoying a feeling of well-being and warmth. Outside I could hear the whirling roar of the wind. The storm had worsened, and though it prevented me from leaving, it might also mean I was safe for the moment.

I heard a knock at the hut's main door and sat up, terrified it was Ariel. Had I slept too long? Perhaps the soup Domick had given me had been laced with sleep potion.

"Who is it?" Domick asked from the other room.

"It's me. Roland," said another voice. I did not know the name. I heard Domick unlatch the door.

"Is Louis here?" asked the newcomer. I crawled out of the bed, crossed quietly to the door, and listened.

"He hasn't come yet," said Domick. "Where is Rushton?"

"He didn't turn up, though I near froze my eyebrows off waiting," said Roland, sounding aggrieved. "Alad says there is some sort of search going on at the house. Guess who has run away now?"

"Elspeth Gordie," Domick said. My heart began to thump wildly. There was a surprised silence.

"How could you know that?" Roland demanded.

"Because she's here," said Domick. "I was out getting wood when I saw her stumbling about like a blind ewe. I locked her in there. She says she came through the drains under the maze, but I don't know how she could know about them."

"She could not have come that way," said Roland. "Alad said Ariel's beasts are out, all around the house."

"From the look of her knees, it is true just the same," said Domick. "You might take a look at them when she wakes. They could use healing."

"We have other concerns," said Roland impatiently. "I want to know what we are to do about the Druid's man. He was supposed to meet with Rushton, but he turns up dead. How are we going to explain that?"

"Rushton will have to tell Henry Druid the truth," said Domick. "The man got himself caught. The question is, did he mention Rushton?"

Roland gave a grunt. "Fortunately, we won't have to explain anything to the Druid until spring, for tonight's snowfall will certainly close off the pass."

"I wish Louis were here," Domick said.

"That old nutter," Roland snapped.

"Well, he was the first to help Rushton," Domick said defensively. "And I know he has spent some time with her." I imagined him gesturing toward my door.

There was another silence.

I debated what to do. It sounded like these two and Louis Larkin were allies of Rushton. But where did the Druid fit in? Was Rushton working for him? He had told me that he had no interest in digging up the past, but Alexi had indicated the Druid was after the same thing he was.

"We ought to look for Rushton," Roland said.

"He said to wait and do nothing," Domick said.

"If Rushton's in trouble, I'm not going to sit back and do nothing."

"We don't even know if he *is* in trouble," Domick insisted.

A log in the fire cracked loudly, and I heard the sound of boots outside. There was a knock, and the outer door opened.

"Louis!" Domick sounded relieved.

"Where's Rushton?" Roland asked swiftly.

"They've taken him prisoner," Louis said in an angry growl. "Alexi and Vega and that demon's whelp, Ariel. They think he helped Elspeth Gordie to escape."

My heart plummeted. Impulsively, I unlocked the door.

For a moment, all was still, like a wax display. Louis, warmly clad with snow melting and dripping in a pool at his feet, and Domick and a man, Roland, near the fire. We all stared at one another, then Domick made a little warding-off movement that unfroze the tableau.

"I locked that," he said faintly.

"You!" Louis said, and to my astonishment, a look of anger filled his face as he stepped threateningly toward me. "You have some explainin' to do!" he growled. "Why do th' Council seek ye?"

"The Council?" Domick echoed.

Louis flicked him a quick quelling glance. "Aye, th' Council. Two Councilmen came up tonight. They have a permit to remove Elspeth Gordie. They said th' Herder Faction wanted to question ye as well."

I felt my face whiten. The Council wanted me, but I dreaded the fanatical Herders, who had burned my parents, far more.

But there was Rushton to think about. "I had a brother. He was involved in some sedition, and they think I can tell them the names of his accomplices," I said, leaving out a world of detail.

Louis squinted his eyes and looked at me skeptically, but I pretended not to see.

"You say they have Rushton? Where?" I asked.

No one answered.

"Look, Rushton *did* help me tonight," I said urgently. "He told me to hide in the silo, but I got lost in the storm."

"Why would he help you?" Roland asked sharply.

I looked at him helplessly, for I did not know that myself.

"She is not important now," said Domick. "We can deal with her later. I don't know how she undid that lock, but I'll tie her up in there and then we can talk."

"No!" I shouted. "Rushton helped me, and now I want to help him."

"Do you know what Rushton is doing here?" Louis asked very carefully.

I hesitated, and then shook my head. "He wouldn't tell me. He said it would put other people in danger. His friends—you, I suppose," I added soberly.

"Where have they got him?" Roland asked Louis.

"Somewhere outside Obernewtyn. It would have to be close," Louis said.

"How could they get outside Obernewtyn in this storm?" Roland demanded. "And why would they bother? They can interrogate him just as well in the doctor's chamber."

His words sparked my memory of the passage concealed behind the doctor's fireplace. Coming from it,

Alexi and the others had been outside and they had spoken of the Zebkrahn machine. "I think I know where they have taken him," I said, trying to contain my excitement.

Louis looked at me, his eyes faded with age and watering from the cold but sharp as a knife. "An' where would that be?" he asked noncommittally.

Seeing that I must trust them if I wanted to be trusted, I told them nearly everything I had seen and heard that night in the doctor's chamber. The three men exchanged a long glance, and then Louis said, "Selmar once mentioned something about a track leading from a secret tunnel out of the grounds. The place is fair riddled with tunnels and hidden passages. And maybe it comes out close to a cave or rift where they found this Zebkrahn. The best way to find it would be to start in the doctor's chamber, but the house is in an uproar."

"We have to search outside the grounds for the other end of the passage," Roland said.

But Louis was still looking at me. "Perhaps you can find him," he said quietly.

The other two stared at him in bewilderment.

"You can ask him where he is and what he wants us to do," Louis continued.

My heart skipped a beat at the knowledge in his look. Slowly, I nodded. "It will be better if I can get outside the walls of Obernewtyn first. The closer I am, the better. And I won't be able to do anything until the snowstorm stops."

"My bones tell me that this storm has near worn out its malice. The minute it stops, I will take ye to the farm gate."

Realization dawned on Domick's face. "You . . . you are like Selmar was before," he said.

That was something I had not guessed, and it made what had been done to her even more of a tragedy. "I'll help," I said. "But I don't have much courage."

Louis spoke briskly. "There's strong an' weak in th' world. If yer born without courage, ye mun look in yerself an' find it. From what Selmar said, this place is a good step from here, so I'd say it mun be closer to the front gate of Obernewtyn. We'll head that way."

Roland stiffened. "What about the granite outcrops? No one bothers going near them because they are all jagged stone and brambles, but there could easily be a cave in them."

"It is the most likely spot for a cave," Domick agreed.

"Well then," said Louis, looking at me. "We'll start out walking in the direction of the outcrops as ye seek Rushton. I'll show ye when we get outside the gate, and from the sound of things, that won't be long, fer the storm is fading." We all listened a moment, and it was true that it was growing quieter.

"This is it, then, isn't it?" Domick said, bright spots of color in his cheeks. He grabbed his coat, then he handed me the one Rushton had given me.

Roland pulled on his own coat and said to Domick, "You get the swords and arrows from the weapons cache, and I will call the others together. Then we will come after you two." He nodded to Louis.

"Let's gan," Louis said to me, and hauled open the door. A few flakes of snow whirled in on the icy air, but the night was again still, the land glowing white and the sky black. We parted from the other two without any more words, and Louis took the lead, walking swiftly and unerringly over what the snow made a trackless, featureless terrain that went as far as my eyes could see. After some time, I saw the wall looming up in the bleakness, a gray band between the black sky and the white ground. As we walked along it, I asked him how he had known about me.

He glanced back. "Selmar told me just before she tried to escape fer th' last time. Most of her was long ago lost, but there were moments when she came to herself. She said you were like her, but stronger. She dreamed that you were coming, and that your coming would change everything."

I did not know what to say to that.

Louis stopped when we reached the farm gate. He unlocked it with a key, and after we had gone through, he locked it from the other side. Then he looked at me expectantly. Knowing what he wanted, and feeling strangely self-conscious, I was about to farseek when I remembered what had happened the last time I had loosed my mind on the farms. The Zebkrahn machine had caught hold of me. On the other hand, if it was being used to interrogate Rushton, surely it could not also be able to entrap roaming minds. I shrugged, knowing I had no real choice but to try. I sent my mind out, but after a time, I breathed a sigh.

"I can't feel him. But maybe the cave wall is blocking me. I have to get closer."

Louis led me along a snowy track that followed the outside of the wall. After some time, he stopped and pointed. I saw the dim outline of several high stone mounds, gray against a slightly lighter sky. I tried again

214

to farseek Rushton, and this time I felt something. The old man saw the look on my face and leaned forward eagerly.

"It was just the merest flicker, but I think the others were right. I think he's there. I need to go closer."

Louis nodded, then his face fell and he cursed. "I am a blatherin' fool! I locked the gate without thinking, an' th' others will not be able to come after us."

"Go back then," I urged. "I can see the outcrops now, so I don't need any guiding."

"I will, but ye be careful, lass. Find him, but dinna go close enough to be caught," Louis warned. "We'll need ye to guide us."

"You be careful, too," I said.

Louis nodded, and without ceremony turned to hurry back along the wall.

✦ 25 ✦

I WOKE TO the dense whiteness of a blinding snow-storm. The events before my fall were tumbled together in a wild kaleidoscopic dream. The last thing I remembered clearly was that I had been walking toward the granite outcrops as the snow fell more and more thickly, until all at once I could see nothing at all. Then I was running. And now here I was, lying in a deep ditch, my head aching and a numbness creeping over my limbs.

I forced myself to sit up, and all at once I remembered what had made me run. I had seen the glimmer of eyes, and the memory of what Ariel's wolves had done to Sharna had sent me into a headlong, mindless flight. That was when I had fallen.

I climbed out of the ditch as carefully as I could for the sake of my aching head, only belatedly realizing that I might have crawled into the mouth of the very wolf that had sent me hurtling into the ditch in the first place. Fortunately, there was no wolf in sight. Brushing off the snow and stamping my feet hard, I looked around and wondered how long I had been unconscious. The fact that I had not frozen suggested it could not have been long. Then I thought of Rushton, and a sense of urgency filled me.

I heard a noise behind me and turned to find myself looking into a pair of gleaming yellow eyes. I would have run, but terror drained the strength from my legs.

Then a familiar voice spoke inside my mind.

"Greetings, ElspethInnle."

"Maruman?" I whispered incredulously.

"It is I," he answered.

I burst out laughing, half in relief and half in hysteria.

"You fell," Maruman observed disapprovingly as he came closer.

I felt the laughter rise again but fought it down. "How on earth did you get here?" I asked.

"You did not come, so I/Maruman came," he sent. He sounded offended, but there was no time to soothe him.

"I could not come to you," I told him. "I have been a captive until this very day. But now I have escaped, and I have to help a friend who is in trouble."

He mulled that over for a moment, then sent in a less haughty tone, "This night I came over the poisoned snowy ground in the wheeled creature drawn by the equines. Funaga rode within. I came because I saw that your nameshape was in their thoughts. But when the horses stopped, I could not sense you anywhere. I slunk into the house, and then I slept and dreamed of you."

"You were clever to find me," I sent quickly. "But there is no time for mindspeak."

"Your friend?" Maruman inquired with pointed politeness.

"He helped me; now I must help him," I sent.

Maruman's thoughts showed he approved of that, at least. "Where is Innle friend?" he asked.

I explained that I did not know exactly where Rushton was. "He's in a cave nearby. I was walking to the mounds of stone, but I fell and now I don't know where I am."

"I will lead you to the mounds of stone," Maruman told me.

I told him cautiously that I thought it would be better if he stayed behind and waited for me, but he fixed me with a penetrating look.

"Innle must seek the darkness, and I/Maruman must go with her to watch the moon." I shivered and felt a mad impulse to forget everything and flee as fast as I could from the mountains and from all of the dangers and mysteries that lay within them.

But then I thought of Rushton and his cool green eyes, and knew there was a debt I must pay.

"Come then," I sent. "But we have to move quickly. I have wasted too much time here."

I had run right by the mounds of stone, as it transpired, and as we retraced my steps, Maruman proved to be an expert guide. Twice he prevented me from stumbling into holes filled with snow. Another time he stopped me from walking onto wafer-thin ice covering a frozen pool of water and camouflaged by a dusting of snow.

So when he stopped just ahead of me, fur fluffed, I froze immediately.

"What is it?" I asked.

He told me that his nose had caught the faint spoor of wolf. I picked up a stout stick before we continued, but saw almost immediately the large humped shapes of granite.

"That is where we will find my friend," I told Maruman.

Given my delays, I had no idea if Louis Larkin and the others had already come and gone, but I did not want to risk using the energy it would require to perform an open farsensing so close to the Zebkrahn machine. First I needed to locate Rushton, and a mental probe shaped to find him would use far less energy. I waited until we reached the bramble-covered rocks that formed a spiky barrier around the mounded stone humps, then I closed my eyes and loosed my mind. I strove about the granite hillocks and several times felt something, but the contact was too slight for me to know if it was Rushton.

"There is danger here," Maruman observed. Then he gave a low, eerie call, and his spine twitched convulsively. "Forever and forever is pain . . . ," he yowled, his eyes whirling.

"Please, not now," I begged. But it was a useless plea, for Maruman's fits were not his to control.

"Here is darkness, ElspethInnle, but it is not the same darkness you must seek out and end." He was trembling from head to toe now and I longed to gather him in my arms, but I knew from experience that he would attack me tooth and claw if I did.

I stared at him, wondering how I could look after Maruman and search for Rushton at the same time.

"The flies!" Maruman shrieked suddenly into my mind, then he swooned sideways and lay still. It was almost a relief to be able to wrap his limp form up in my coat. I laid him in a small hollow in a rock, fairly sure he would not wake until I returned. Then I clambered as fast as I could over the bramble-covered rocks, toward the larger hillocks in their midst.

Five minutes later, I was in a narrow flat space between the prickly scree and the mounds of stone. Almost at once, I found the entrance to a cave, though I saw no sign of any tunnel leading back to Obernewtyn.

· 26 ·

THE CAVE ENTRANCE was hidden behind a rockfall. Its placement was too convenient, concealing the cave perfectly without blocking it off. I had no doubt that it had been purposefully placed, though only the machines of the Beforetimers could have shifted such weight.

Up close, I realized that the rockfall and the hillock itself were not true granite at all but some kind of smooth, hard stone the likes of which I had never seen.

I entered the cave and found that it was a tunnel burrowing into the largest of the mounds. I could see light ahead and approached with trepidation, but it was only a great shimmering cluster of insects gathered on a damp patch of rock. The light they gave out revealed the tunnel for some distance, and then I found a lantern hanging from a peg of wood that had been driven into a crack in the wall. It was the first certain proof that someone was using the cavern.

I continued, moving as swiftly as I could without making any noise, and keeping close to the walls. All at once, the walls and ceiling went from being something like raw stone to being smooth and perfectly squared, as if a stonemason had dressed and polished them. This and the machine Alexi had spoken of indicated that I was inside a Beforetime building—or what remained of one.

I passed another lantern and tried again to farseek Rushton. Now that I was within the mound of stone there was less interference, and for a moment I sensed him clearly.

He was in pain.

The tunnel began to slope down slightly, and here and there the smooth surface was broken. In one place, a thick pool of multicolored ooze was coming from a crack running up the wall. I kept well away from the slimy mess in case it was tainted. The tunnel curved, and I blinked at the flood of light ahead. Soon, the path swelled out and curved into an enormous, brightly lit cavern. The light came not from lanterns but from a round white sphere on top of a pole. It hummed faintly, and my skin rose into gooseflesh because this was a Beforetime artifact that *someone had brought to life.*

There was no one in sight. Entering the chamber warily, I saw that all around were silvery boxes of varying sizes, many higher than my head. Buttons and gleaming jewel-colored lights covered the surfaces of what must surely have been Beforetime machines. One had been forced away from the wall. It was very large, with a flat extension coming out one side and many thin colored strands running hither and thither. I wondered if this was the Zebkrahn machine. But if so, where was Alexi? Or Rushton? I looked closely at the machine, but I could not tell whether it was operating.

There were three open doorways in addition to the one I had come through. One way was smooth and perfectly shaped, but the other two were cracked and crumbling, both angling down. Hearing nothing when

I listened at each of them, I decided to go through the undamaged doorway. The path leading from it was dark, for no lantern had been left hanging and there were none of the shining insects. I was on the verge of turning back when I thought I heard a voice ahead. Then a little farther on and around a corner I saw light again. It was another lantern hanging in an alcove, but as I reached for it I stifled a cry of fright and staggered back, for two eyes flared at me.

It took me a long moment to take in that the eyes did not move or glisten. My heart was still pounding as I went closer and took the lantern. I saw then that the eyes belonged to a stuffed Guanette bird mounted on a shelf of stone. Even in death, the massive bird's bright, round eyes seemed penetrating, and I wondered in disgust who would kill and stuff something so rare and lovely.

I heard a sound behind me and whirled, but I could see nothing. I went across to another alcove, where there was a bed set again the wall. Then I saw a movement and realized with a shock that it was occupied. "Rushton?" I whispered.

The person lying on the bed stirred and turned toward me. To my astonishment, I saw that it was Cameo!

The light bathed her face as I approached, and her skin glowed marble white so that the blackness under her eyes looked like crescents of ink. Her eyes flickered open. "Elf?" she murmured, but vaguely. It was strange and terrible to hear her using Jes's nickname for me, but I reached out and touched her face. She frowned and said more strongly, "Elspeth?"

"I'm here," I whispered.

Consternation crossed her features, bringing them to life. "No! You mustn't be here. He . . . he wants you. I heard him say it. You must go now."

"Don't talk," I begged.

She fell back and closed her eyes. "I knew you would come," she whispered.

But too late, I thought to myself.

"Not too late!" she protested, and I gasped, for she had read my thought. Then I saw that she had heard my realization as well, for she said, "I don't know why, but somehow the pain made me . . . able to hear better. But I still couldn't do what they wanted. I'm not strong enough. But while they used their machines, I had a true dream. I dreamed there is something you have to do. You alone. I dreamed it was more important than anything else in the world. It has something to do with this place and with the map that Alexi seeks. The map that . . . shows the way to a terrible power. . . . He does not realize how terrible it is, and it would not stop him if he did know."

"A . . . terrible power?" I echoed, thinking of all the nightmarish stories I had heard of the capacity of the Beforetimers for violence and destruction.

"Worse," Cameo whispered. "Worse than you can possibly imagine. The map shows the way to the very machines that caused the Great White."

"No!" I gasped.

Her eyes fluttered, and I saw the effort it took for her to go on. "You have to stop them from finding the machines, Elspeth. You have to find them first and make sure no one can ever use them." The veins in her neck stood out like cords.

"I can't do that," I said, my mind whirling.

224

"You can, for you are the Seeker," she said.

"Please," I rasped, and discovered that tears were running down my face. For Cameo was dying. *It is my fault*, I thought. All along it was me they really wanted.

"You came," she whispered.

I fell to my knees by her bed and cried while she stroked my hair with a hand no heavier than a breath of air. Then her hand was still.

I wept bitter tears until a laugh echoed down the passages and penetrated the fog of sorrow that had enveloped me. I stood up. I knew that laugh, and it dried all the tears and sorrow in me, leaving a rime of brittle determination. I set off down a hallway that led deeper into the structure, vowing that Ariel and the others would pay for what they had done to Cameo.

When I got closer to the source of his laughter, I saw there was light ahead. I extinguished my lantern and set it down before continuing.

I had been creeping along for several minutes when Madam Vega suddenly spoke, so near that it sent ice sifting over my skin. I inched forward until I could see into another room, and listened hard.

"You are collaborating with the Druid, aren't you?" Madam Vega asked. "You need not answer. What the Druid's man told us reveals that much. Did you really suppose we would allow you to come in and take what we have schemed and killed to gain? I suppose the old man promised to help you take Obernewtyn for yourself, if only to rid himself of us? As if he has the power for anything but skulking in the wilderness."

"The Council does not allow a defective to inherit, but it will allow a bastard son to do so," said Rushton.

My heart leapt at hearing him speak. I regretted that

I had not tried to farseek Louis before I had entered the stone hillock, for I had clearly arrived before him. I decided to go back outside to wait for the others, but Madam Vega's next words froze me in my tracks.

"There is no proof that you are Michael Seraphim's illegitimate son," she said in an amused tone. "Your mother could easily have lied."

"There are my father's letters to her, and my appearance," Rushton said. "When my mother sent me here, she thought my father still lived. She thought he would see himself in my face, and so she gave me no letter or token to show the man she sent me to find. Nor did she tell me that he was my father."

"Too bad Michael Seraphim was dead before you arrived," Madam Vega sneered.

I had listened to what they were saying with growing amazement. That Rushton was Michael Seraphim's illegitimate son would explain much, but would he really ally himself with Henry Druid in order to make a claim for Obernewtyn?

"I will enjoy killing you," Madam Vega said softly when Rushton made no response. "As long as you were ignorant of your true status, it amused me to let you live. Even to indulge you. But you have proven troublesome and ungrateful. Now, there are a few questions I want answered."

"I will tell you nothing," Rushton grated.

There was the sound of a sharp blow.

"Have some respect," Ariel said silkily.

Creeping around a bank of machines, I saw Madam Vega, Ariel, and what looked to be the tip of Rushton's boot. He was lying on a metal tray before an immense machine, and my heart seized at the sight. *This* must be the Zebkrahn machine, I realized.

I was just summoning up a probe to reach out to Rushton when a voice spoke behind me, soft with menace.

"How obliging of you to come to us," murmured Alexi. Then something heavy crashed into the base of my skull, and a wave of blackness filled my mind.

Alexi and Madam Vega were talking when I woke. I was lying down and bound hand, foot, and throat. I kept my eyes closed and listened.

"Why did you have to hit her so hard?" the woman complained. "You could have killed her!"

"She will not die," Alexi said dismissively.

"What about *him*, then?" Ariel said. "He fainted, and you said he wouldn't. Now we'll have to wait till he wakes to finish questioning him."

"I'm not interested in him any longer," Alexi said coldly. "We have the girl."

"Nevertheless, I want to know how they are connected," said Madam Vega. "Rushton accepted pain rather than revealing the whereabouts of this girl, and it is obvious now that he *did* help her to escape."

"We will ask the girl," Alexi said after a thoughtful pause. "She will respond swiftly enough after we threaten him, if they are allies."

"He'll talk if we use her as a lever," Ariel said eagerly. "You should have seen his face when we came to that mess the wolves had made in the courtyard. At first, we thought it was her that had been torn apart. Rushton seemed to go mad. That's why I had to shoot him."

"I'm not interested in this," Alexi snapped. "I want that map."

"We will have it soon," Madam Vega said soothingly. "The girl will locate it for us. And what power we will have over the Council once we have Beforetime weaponmachines. They will refuse us nothing. And if they displease us, we will give them a demonstration."

I felt a caress on my face and opened my eyes.

"Awake . . . ," purred Alexi, his face close to mine, his eyes dark. I shuddered as far away from him as my bindings would allow, and he laughed wildly until Madam Vega took his hand and bade him calm himself.

"We don't want to make any mistakes. We cannot afford another Selmar."

"I will get the diaries," Alexi said, ignoring her admonition. He turned, addressing Ariel as he left. "She is sweating. That might affect the machine. Clean her."

"I am not his servant," Ariel hissed.

"Be silent and do as you were bidden," Madam Vega snapped.

Sullenly, Ariel wiped my face with a cool cloth. "Crazy as a loon, he is. Lud, but he's creepy with those monster eyes," he muttered under his breath.

"You forget yourself, Ariel," Madam Vega said. "Without Alexi, all of my plans will come to nothing. Only he understands these infernal machines. Now come with me."

I heard their voices receding in the distance and bitterly cursed my carelessness. I had practically given myself as a gift to them. And they meant to use me to find the weaponmachines that caused the Great White. Would it be any use to tell them what Cameo had said? I could not think so, remembering the relish in Madam

Vega's voice when she had spoken of giving a demonstration of power to the Council. I knew I must not help them to find Marisa's map or I would be directly responsible for unleashing the horrors of the Great White on the world again. Bleakly, I prayed for the courage to keep silent, but the thought of being tortured terrified me.

I heard a groan and knew it meant Rushton was waking up. I decided I must tell him that his friends were searching for him, and that they had a good idea of his location. Now that I looked about me, I saw that I was strapped to the extended table of the machine I had seen earlier. I could not turn my head far because of the binding about my throat, but I could see a hand tied to a chair. It moved, straining against the bindings.

"Rushton?" I whispered.

"Elspeth?" he croaked. "I thought you were dead."

"It was Sharna the wolves killed," I said with a stab of renewed grief.

"I thought they had torn you apart," Rushton said again. "I wanted to kill Ariel. Instead, he shot me with a bolt from his crossbow." He stifled a groan, and I saw that he was again straining against his bonds.

"Rushton, I need to tell you . . ." I broke off, hearing the approach of footsteps. It was Alexi, and Madam Vega returned with Ariel a moment later. Among them, they had brought scrolled papers and maps and parchments, as well as several fat, battered-looking books.

"We will begin with the diaries," Alexi announced, taking one of the books and staring down into my eyes. "I wish you to use your Misfit abilities to learn where Marisa hid a map she made. I know you have the power to hear the thoughts she had when she scribed

229

her notes. If you cooperate, I will not need to use the Zebkrahn."

"You will kill me, whatever happens," I said, thinking I had to give Louis and the others time to find us.

"You will tell me!" Alexi raged. He turned to the machine, and Vega hovered behind him with anxious eyes.

"Be careful, Alexi," she warned.

"I will teach her not to defy me," he snarled. He did something to the buttons, and several colored lights began to pulsate. The machine hummed very faintly, and Alexi took up a bowl-shaped helmet and fitted it over my head, his strange black eyes burning down at me.

All at once, I felt a faint buzzing in my head. It was only slightly distracting, and my spirits lifted. If this was the extent of their torture, the secret of the map's whereabouts would be safe with me. I wondered suddenly if Marisa had even known the terrible capability of the weaponmachines she had located. I remembered that cold, enigmatic face in the portrait and thought it must be so.

"Even if you find what you want, the Council will not let you rule them," Rushton said.

"He's just trying to get you mad," Ariel sneered.

Alexi turned his hot, mad gaze on Ariel, who visibly quailed. "I'll kill you if you say anything else that annoys me," the man hissed.

"Concentrate on the girl," snapped Madam Vega, giving Ariel a warning look. Alexi came back to the machine and turned a knob, and the buzzing in my head increased sharply. The sensation was still a long way from being painful, yet I thought uneasily of Cameo and Selmar. Selmar, who had been more like me than I could have guessed. Was it this machine that had broken her mind?

Alexi took the diary, opened it, and held it in front of my eyes. I tried not to look at the crabbed scribing, which I recognized from the maps and books in the doctor's chamber, but the nearness of the diary was such that I could hear the faintest whisper of the woman's thoughts. I strengthened my shield.

"I have dreamed of the power that will come to me," Alexi said. "It is my destiny, and Marisa had no right to keep it from me." He moved a lever on the machine, and the buzzing increased. It was uncomfortable enough to begin eroding the solidity of my shield. Again I heard the whisper of Marisa's thoughts rising from the diary like a scent. Complex calculations. The desire for a certain book. An unkind thought about her baby son, whom she suspected of being dull-witted. Irritation with her husband.

"Open your mind to her," Alexi commanded, and again the buzzing increased. Now there was pain. I could tolerate it, but there would be more, I knew, and worse. What if I could not hold out?

Fear made me grope for Rushton's mind. If I could just speak with him, I might find courage enough to endure.

"Think of Marisa," Alexi commanded.

My mental probe found Rushton's mind, but it was blocked. I despaired for a moment, but then I realized that his mind was not consciously shielded. Nor had he a natural block. The barrier I encountered was unlike any I had felt. It was like a thick wall of cloud or mist. I gathered my strength and arrowed my way through it into his mind. Distantly I heard him moan.

"What is the matter with him?" Vega asked.

"He's fainted again," Ariel said contemptuously.

But he was wrong. Rushton had retreated into his thoughts to deal with my intrusion. Quickly I identified myself.

"It was *you.*" I heard Rushton's thought and, with astonishment, recognized the mind of my rescuer. At least, his mind seemed part of the entity that had helped me get free from the Zebkrahn once before. But I could tell he had no Misfit ability.

Seeming to guess my puzzlement, Rushton explained. "There are many among my friends who have mental abilities like yours, and though none are as powerful as you, they are able to combine their strength. Somehow they use my mind to focus their energies, and carry me with them. If I had succeeded in making my claim on Obernewtyn, I would have made it a refuge for them."

I told Rushton he must not give up, for his friends were on their way with help.

"My friends?" he echoed.

Swiftly I shared with him everything that had happened since we parted last. It took but a moment, because I used mental pictures rather than words. I read in his mind that he was unaware that the weaponmachines sought by Alexi and the others were those that had caused the Great White. I chose not to burden him with the knowledge, though he asked if I could do what Alexi wanted.

Before I could answer, the effect of the Zebkrahn increased dramatically. I tried to withdraw from Rushton's mind, but he held me.

"Let me go!" I begged. It would have been easy enough to tear free, but he would be hurt.

"I can help you endure," he said. "Draw on me." I warned him that he would share my pain if I stayed inside his mind, but he insisted. "If you give them what they want, they will kill us both anyway, so I help myself in helping you."

"This is taking too long," I heard Ariel say impatiently. He reached up to adjust the machine, but this time there was no increase in the pain. Had the machine reached its limit? I prayed so, for on the other side of my mental barrier, I could sense Marisa's thoughts clamoring.

"Don't be afraid," Rushton told me. Then I heard him moan and realized with horror that he was shielding me from the worst of the pain. I did not know how it was possible, and yet he was doing it.

"What is wrong with him?" Vega snapped.

Alexi sprang forward and looked into my face. "He's helping her!" he screamed. "Kill him, Vega."

"No!" I cried.

His brows drew together in triumph. "Tell me where the map is or I will kill him," he whispered. I wrenched my mind from Rushton's with a scream.

"Vega, get a knife," Alexi instructed. He looked back at me. "Tell me or he will die."

"Elspeth!" Rushton shouted.

In that moment, the block that separated me from Marisa's thoughts was as thin as a web. I saw right through it and knew where the map was. It was hidden in plain sight, carved into the front doors of Obernewtyn. Then, as my mind began to buckle under the assault of the machine, I saw a vision of a dark chasm in the ground from which rose a thick brownish smoke, and I knew I was seeing the very place indicated on Marisa's map.

Terrified at what else I would see, I found the strength to block the vision and push Marisa from me.

"Very well, kill him," Alexi snarled.

I threw back my head and saw Madam Vega's hand raise the knife. "No!" I begged.

"Tell me," Alexi whispered.

"We come," said an unknown voice in my mind. Startled, I realized Rushton's friends must be within the stone hillock.

"Tell me!" Alexi shouted.

I hesitated. I could not tell him where the map was. That was too high a price for either my life or Rushton's.

Alexi's eyes narrowed, seeming to divine my thought. "All right. Do it."

Madam Vega lifted her arm slowly.

I heard running footsteps, and at the same time, the machine seemed to be overheating. There was the sound of an explosion, and a shower of sparks fell on my boot and onto my bare and grazed knees. I jerked and kicked as best I could.

Vega's hand paused before the downward blow. She looked at Alexi, and he nodded.

There was a terrible pain in my legs and feet, and I could smell smoke.

Then something inside my head crackled violently; a power stirred in me completely unlike any other ability I possessed. All at once, I knew that Rosamunde had spoken the truth: Jes had killed that soldierguard, *and I knew how.*

Whatever I had roused came from the deepest void of my mind, like a serpent uncoiling to strike. I felt a sense of exaltation at the knowledge that I could control such a terrible power. Madam Vega drove the knife downward, but I struck first, swatting her hand away and plowing a terrible furrow through her mind. She screamed horribly.

I felt flames burning my legs and feet. The smell reminded me of the day my mother and father died.

Dimly, I saw people running and shouting.

"Is she alive?" asked a voice I knew but could not recognize.

Am I? I wondered, and a dark wind swept me away.

✦ 27 ✦

"YER NOWT WELL enough!" Matthew said stubbornly. The look on his face told me what I already knew. I looked haggard even after all this time.

"It might be better . . . ," Dameon said diplomatically, but I would not let him finish.

"Stay here and miss this mysterious meeting? Not on your life," I said. I sat back after that outburst, feeling the now-familiar weakness roll over me. It was still incredible to think the machine had taken so much from me. That, and unleashing the strange power I had tapped in myself. I had been unconscious for days after.

"Ye look different," Matthew said. And I felt different, stronger somehow, despite my physical weakness and the scars. Even now I could feel the tingle in the depth of my mind that told me the power was there, waiting.

"So *you* would be different if some machine had been inside your head," I snapped.

He grinned.

"Where is Rushton?" I asked casually.

Matthew looked quickly at Dameon, but the empath's face remained as inscrutable as ever. I felt a stirring of resentment that Rushton had not come by to visit. Matthew had told me that Louis and the others had freed Rushton and he had beaten and smothered the flames that had engulfed my lower legs. Both Alexi and Madam Vega were dead—Alexi with an arrow to the heart and Vega without a mark on her. Louis guessed she had fallen and hit her head in the commotion. Ariel had fled, and had surely perished in the savage blizzard that had come that night.

It was known now by all those who dwelt at Obernewtyn that Rushton was its legal master and that the mysterious doctor was his defective half brother. None doubted the claim, and the new Master of Obernewtyn spoke openly of taking it to the Council-court to have the matter formally recognized.

I was amazed at how many different varieties of mental prowess there were among the Misfits at Obernewtyn, and at the fact that I had never realized it. But, of course, I had kept my mind tightly leashed after my first encounter with the Zebkrahn machine. And most of the Misfits had minimal abilities; Roland, Domick, and a few others were the exception. But type and strength of ability did not matter to Rushton, who had none save the curious ability to host a merge of minds. In a way, it seemed to me that his desire to turn Obernewtyn into a refuge echoed this ability. The meeting I wanted to attend was meant to outline his plans in detail.

Matthew and Dameon felt I was not fit enough to attend. I insisted that the numbness and pain in my mind had gone, but I was still very weak and the burns on my feet and legs were yet to heal fully. Rushton had left word that I was not to get up until I was completely recovered. And still he had not come to see me.

"He's the master here now," Matthew said, as if answering my thought.

"No doubt he is too busy to tell me himself that I must not come to his meeting," I said. I had meant to say it lightly, but I heard a flash of anger in my voice and realized that I only wanted to go because Rushton wanted to stop me.

Dameon said gently, "He *did* come to see you several times, Elspeth. But you were always asleep, and he would not let us wake you."

"Of course," I said as casually as possible, ashamed to think he was privy to my pettiness when we all knew how busy Rushton was. And after all, Rushton did not know I had stopped Vega from killing him. In truth, I did not want anyone to know that. The fact that I had the capacity to kill with my mind was hardly likely to endear me to anyone.

"We've decided we're going to stay," Matthew said. "Rushton's going to make Obernewtyn a secret refuge for people like us. He has plans."

"I know that." I snapped. Dameon was staring at me with an odd expression on his face, and I felt a blush rise to my cheeks at the thought that he was sensing the muddled roil of my emotions.

"What about Henry Druid? Does he have a role in this great plan?" I asked. Rushton had met the renegade Herder several years before, when he had stumbled into his camp, on his way to Obernewtyn at the request of his dead mother. Instead of being killed or made prisoner, Rushton had been allowed to go free, on the condition that he aided the old man in acquiring some of the forbidden Beforetime books said to be hidden at Obernewtyn.

Once Rushton arrived at the mountain valley, he learned that Michael Seraphim had died. Still puzzled as to why his mother had insisted on him bringing news of her death to a stranger, he had accepted Madam Vega's offer of employment as overseer with the aim of finding out more about Michael Seraphim. Alexi had guessed the truth the moment he saw Rushton, and they meant to keep him close in case the truth about Stephen Seraphim was ever revealed. Madam Vega had done her best to ingratiate herself with him, though she had not told him the truth about his father. It was Louis Larkin who had done that. Rushton had stayed on, hoping to meet his half brother, who was kept mysteriously out of sight. Finally, he had discovered the truth and knew that he had a legitimate claim to Obernewtyn.

But by now he had developed an alliance with Domick and Roland and other Misfits with forbidden abilities, and he had conceived of turning Obernewtyn into a secret refuge. So he had to be very careful about how he established his claim. He must control the process. He also needed to resolve his bargain with Henry Druid. He did not want to find himself at odds with the old man, so he had decided to provide him with several valuable books from the library before severing contact.

But would that satisfy the former Herder? If he was as voracious about forbidden knowledge as he sounded, he would not easily give up his search for weapon-machines. My thoughts shifted to the magnificent carvings on the doors to Obernewtyn. It was a great pity to destroy such craftsmanship, but I could see no other way to get rid of the map they concealed.

"What about the doctor?" I asked.

"I don't think Rushton is quite sure what to do with

him," Dameon said in an amused voice. "He really is rather harmless. It turns out he was using garbled herb lore on the people he treated, and the worst he would have done is give someone a bad bellyache. Roland is trying to teach him some real herb lore, but the doctor is slow and Roland is so impatient."

Looking at my friends, I thought this business had wrought a change in them, too. Dameon seemed quieter and older, while Matthew carried the scar left by Cameo's death in the sadness I sometimes saw in his face. Yet they were more certain of themselves, more purposeful. Perhaps because Rushton had offered them a place in his world.

I found myself yawning and knew I did not really want to go to the meeting. I grinned at their relief when I said so.

"Will you stay?" Dameon asked.

"It will be some time before I can think of leaving," I said, sidestepping the question.

Dameon did not press me. In truth, I did not know what I would do. I did not think I would stay at Obernewtyn, for I had a yearning to travel, to see the great sea and the western coast. But it would be as difficult as ever to move from place to place in the Land, even if Rushton provided me with a Normalcy Certificate, as he had promised any of us who wished to leave the mountains.

"Ye mun stay!" Matthew cried, looking disappointed. "Rushton said you're stronger than all of us. He has the notion of starting his own council!"

Dameon nodded, sensing my curiosity and incredulity. "He wants to govern Obernewtyn with the help and advice of a council elected from our ranks. He wants us to work at our abilities and to train others to be better at what we do."

"He wants us to form groups, guilds organized by special abilities," Matthew added.

"And this council will be a sort of guild merge," I quipped.

Dameon's mouth twitched. "A good name. I will suggest it," he said.

I laughed. Then another question occurred to me.

"Speaking of councils, what happened to those Councilmen and the soldierguards that came up here?" To my surprise, Matthew only laughed.

"*There's* a story," he said with a twinkle in his eyes. "Madam Vega made the mistake of leaving the Councilmen to Ariel's tender mercies. He fed them drugged wine and threw them in one of the underground storage chambers."

I gaped.

"By the time they were discovered, it was all over. Rushton got them out and told them what had happened—with a few omissions."

"A few omissions!" I gasped.

Matthew grinned widely, enjoying his audience. "He told them Madam Vega and Alexi had been plotting against the Council, and that they had organized to have the Councilmen knocked out and murdered in case they found out that Stephen Seraphim was defective and their prisoner."

"And they believed him?" I asked.

"With a little empathy," Dameon said with a sly, slow smile.

"Rushton gave them the impression the whole revolt had been meant to free them," Matthew continued.

"They were sick to their stomachs from th' stuff Ariel had given them, and they were only too happy to believe anything they were told by the man who rescued them. Those with empath abilities have been preparing them to rush back to Sutrium after the thaw, and ye can be sure Rushton will have no trouble getting his claim accepted after they prepare the way."

I laughed aloud at the thought of the self-important Councilmen thrown into a storage cupboard. Then I sobered. "What about me?"

"What about you?" Matthew inquired pertly. "You're dead. You ran away during the battle and were almost certainly tragically devoured by wild wolves."

Domick poked his head around the door. "Rushton's coming up."

Dameon and Matthew moved to depart.

"Wait. Don't . . ." *Don't what?* I wondered. *Don't leave me alone with the person who risked his life to help me?* I shook my head at the absurdity, and they went.

Rushton seemed too tall in the turret room that had once been his own chamber. There were faint shadows under his green eyes that told of the long hours he had been spending at reorganizing Obernewtyn, but he looked remarkably content.

"I heard you want to come to the meeting," he said.

I shrugged. "Not really. It was a whim. I hear you have plans," I said.

He didn't seem to hear me. "I feared you would die or wake up senseless like Selmar."

I shrugged again, embarrassed at his intensity. "Well, I didn't," I said with some asperity. "I never thanked you for helping me with the machine that time."

242

He shrugged. "Will you stay?" he asked, rather as Dameon had done.

"I don't know," I said.

"Did they tell you my idea about the guilds? You could stay and help set it up," he offered diffidently.

"What guild would I belong to?" I asked, striving for a lightness I could not seem to feel.

"Choose whichever pleases you. You seem to have every ability save empathy." He smiled. "You are the strongest Misfit here by far, but we're going to bring others up here, too, you know. In secret. You could help to train them. And when we're strong enough, we will force the Council to accept Misfits." He paused. "Stay," he said again when I did not answer.

"I'll stay for a while," I said at last.

"That will do to start," he said cryptically. He glanced through the unshuttered window at the pale wintertime sky. "It will not be easy, I know, to do what I want. But one day, Obernewtyn will be a force in this Land. I will see to that." He smiled down at me, and there was a fierce pride in his face that made it strangely beautiful.

He would be a good leader, I thought after he had gone. Guilds or not, he would remain the Master of Obernewtyn. There was a quality in him that inspired trust and a kind of love. He was born to lead.

People like Rushton never thought much about the past, I thought. It made them impatient. It was left to those like me to remember the past—and doubt.

Deep within, I felt again the tingle of the power I had wakened. Such power must have a purpose. I remembered my vision of a dark, smoke-filled chasm.

I would destroy the map Marisa Seraphim had left showing its whereabouts, but the chasm would remain, as would whatever documents Marisa had used to create her map. Sooner or later, someone would find the chasm. Unless I found it first.

"The Seeker," Cameo had called me. Strangely, the name Maruman and Sharna had called me meant exactly that. Perhaps it was my destiny to find the weapon-machines and somehow disarm them. The thought lay in my mind, and all the restlessness in me seemed to flow toward it. A vague idea became resolve. One day, I would seek the chasm I had seen, and I would find a way to prevent the weaponmachines within from being used.

Cameo had believed I was important—that I had something important to do in the world—and so had Maruman and Sharna. What could be more important than making sure the Great White could never come again?

✦ About the Author ✦

ISOBELLE CARMODY began the first of her highly acclaimed Obernewtyn Chronicles while still in high school. She continued writing while completing a Bachelor of Arts and a journalism cadetship. This series and her short stories have established her at the forefront of fantasy writing in Australia and abroad.

She is the award-winning author of several novels and many series for young readers, including The Legend of Little Fur, the Gateway Trilogy, and the Obernewtyn Chronicles.

She lives with her family, and they divide their time between homes in Australia and the Czech Republic.

How will Elspeth use her growing power?

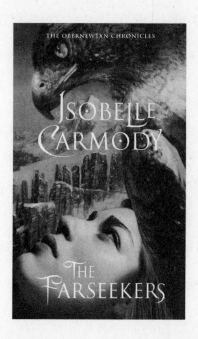

Turn the page for a sneak preview of Elspeth's newfound freedom—available now!

WITHOUT WARNING, THE door was flung open by a wild-eyed Matthew. "Here ye are! I've been searchin' all over for ye!" he said accusingly.

Forgetting his frustration, Matthew hurried over. "Rushton has just come back! An' he's called a guild-merge."

"When?" I asked.

"Now!" Matthew said.

My heart jumped. Something serious must have happened for him to call a guildmerge so abruptly.

"Did he say why?" I asked. I dried my feet quickly and slipped on my boots.

"Nowt a word," Matthew answered, handing me my walking stick. "He was investigatin' a rumor that th' Council meant to establish a soldierguard camp in th' highlands. Do ye suppose . . . ?" he began, aghast at the thought of a camp so close to Obernewtyn. If the Council meant to put a camp in the highlands, it could only be because they intended to tighten their control of the high country.

Rushton was waiting for us in the circular entrance hall. He looked tired, and it was clear from his clothes that he had not bothered to change. I felt a rush of glad-ness at the sight of him, for though Obernewtyn ran smoothly in his absence, I never felt as safe as when he was there.

He met my look with an ambivalent stare. It was almost a challenge. Before I could speak, he sent Matthew to find representatives from the Futuretell guild; then he ushered me toward the guildmerge, matching his steps to my own limping progress.

"What has happened?" I asked.

Rushton turned to look at me. "The Council is showing renewed interest in us. Two men were uplands asking questions about Obernewtyn."

"You think they were from the Council?"

He shrugged angrily. "I know nothing, except that I am tired of my ignorance. Do you remember when I went to claim Obernewtyn in Sutrium?" he asked.

"I remember," I murmured.

"I thought the Council had trusted me when I'd told them that Obernewtyn had been razed in a firestorm and that most of its Misfit inhabitants were dead. Maybe I was wrong. With farseeker or coercer help, I could have made sure. But now . . ."

"Now?" I echoed.

Rushton looked at me, his green eyes glowing with sudden excitement, as if he had resolved some inner doubt. "It's time we found out what the Council is up to. Time we made a move into their territory."

"Sutrium?" I whispered.

"Sutrium," Rushton said.